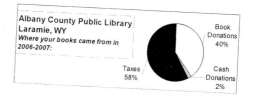

THE
LAST CHRISTMAS RIDE

THE
LAST CHRISTMAS RIDE

a novella

based on a true story

Edie Hand
with Jeffery Addison

CUMBERLAND HOUSE
NASHVILLE, TENNESSEE

A portion of the proceeds from this book will benefit the Edie Hand Foundation. Learn more about the charities at www.ediehandfoundation.org

THE LAST CHRISTMAS RIDE
PUBLISHED BY CUMBERLAND HOUSE PUBLISHING
431 Harding Industrial Drive
Nashville, TN 37211

Copyright © 2007 by Edie Hand and Jeffery Addison

Cover design: James Duncan
Book design: Mary Sanford

Library of Congress Cataloging-in-Publication Data
Hand, Edie, 1951–
  The Last Christmas ride : a novella : based on a true story / by Edie Hand ; with Jeffery Addison.
    p. cm.
  ISBN-13: 978-1-58182-624-1 (alk. paper)
  ISBN-10: 1-58182-624-9 (alk. paper)
  1. Cancer—Patients—Fiction. 2. Christmas stories. 3. Domestic fiction. I. Addison, Jeffery, 1947– II. Title.
  PS3608.A6985L37 2007
  813'.6—dc22

                                                    2007024197

Printed in the United States of America
  2 3 4 5 6 7—12 11 10 09 08 07

For those who have loved and lost
along their rides through life.

To all my family, friends, and colleagues who have
kept my spirit inspired. Thank You!

*"We have no control over life's events but we
do have control over how we respond to them."*

acknowledgments

A very special thank you goes to my friend, Don Keith, who introduced me to Jeffery Addison. It was with his help that *The Last Christmas Ride* was born. I'd like to thank my personal assistant, Kathy Goodwin, for her labor of love on this project. Also my thanks to my precious son, Linc Hand, my mother, Sue Blackburn-Hardesty, my dad, Guy Blackburn, and my sister, Kim Poss-Cook, for sharing the courage in joining me on this sensitive ride. I want to thank my husband, Mark Aldridge, and my extended family and friends, who all contributed ideas that made David, Terry, and Phillip's story a stronger one. You know who you are. There are simply not enough words to express my gratitude to Ron Pitkin, the publisher of Cumberland House, who believed in me and the boys' story. Thank you to my literary agent, Harvey Klinger, and to my business manager, Bob Layne, for encouraging me to never give up! Thanks for the music to Ronnie McDowell, Landri Taylor, Dak Alley, and Dottie Rager.

prologue

My brother Terry came much too early to the end of life's ride.

I am thankful that when the time did come, a few days shy of Christmas, he was where he most wanted to be: at home in the bedroom of the house he built with his own two hands. And he was surrounded by those who loved him most.

It was a special home. Terry Blackburn built it strong, to last. He was a carpenter, a contractor, and he knew what it took to build something that would endure. He hammered in four nails where two would have done just as well. He used carefully selected two-by-sixes for joists and sills and rafters where the typical builder would have happily settled for run-of-the-mill two-by-fours. He used big, flat river stones on the façade and to methodically lay into the floor of the patio.

Terry hauled them up by himself from the creek that ran along the far edge of the property where we all grew up. Then, like an artist mixing his palette, he deliberately matched and set each one by hand. The house had strong beams running across the ceiling of the sunken den. They came from oak logs hewed from trees that he sawed down himself. He hauled them back from the far corner of the home place on one of our grandpa's old wagons, pulled along by two of Terry's horses. His hands bled through his gloves as he handled the stones and placed the beams by himself, but he never seemed to mind. He ignored the pain because he knew that he was building something big and strong and lasting.

My brother earned everything he had in life with

hard work and dogged determination and a get-it-done attitude. He took it for granted that that was the way things were supposed to be done, that perseverance would win out over any obstacle that might be placed in his way.

"If I'm going to all the trouble to build a house, I might as well build it right," Terry announced to us, a broad grin on his handsome face as he strung the lines from stake to stake to mark where he would dig the footing. As usual, he did what he said he would do. "I want this house to be standing here long after I'm dead and gone. Maybe one of my boys will live here with his family someday. And then my grandkids will raise their own young'uns and tell them about how old Grandpa Terry built this place. You know what the Bible says about a house built on sand. This one is built on rock, and it's made out of oak."

When I came back home to visit and as we caught glimpses of his new house rising among the big cedars on the hill, we had no reason to doubt him. At the same time, we never suspected that

Terry's life would be cut so short, that such a strong, full-of-life man would not live to see his grandchild playing on the rock patio of the strong house he built.

Toward the end of his days, I watched sadly, helplessly, as my brother stared at the calendar on the kitchen wall, eyeing a festive red patch of print that marked Christmas Day.

"Terry, you'll have lots more Christmases," I told him, reading his mind.

"Don't think so," he answered as he watched the lights twinkling on the artificial tree my sister and I had erected and decorated for him.

Christmas was easily his favorite holiday, one he still anticipated as eagerly as he had done when we were growing up.

He didn't quite get there.

Terry had a favorite expression he liked to use when we were kids. We would be playing our make-believe games, riding our horses through the pastures around home, building empires and vanquishing enemies who dared threaten the fields and pine thickets around our little Alabama hometown. One of us would say something about being tired of playing or hint that we should probably get on home to supper before Mother got mad at us. We were more afraid of her than of invading Nazi armies or a horde of Mexican banditos sweeping down upon us from up somewhere close to Haleyville.

"The best part of a trip ain't getting to wherever it is that you're going. It's the trip itself," Terry would announce, using a voice that sounded much older than he really was. Then he would grin, make a clicking noise with his tongue, and knee his horse, Polly, in her flanks. Off he would go, whooping all the way, galloping into the dusk with the wind rippling his long, brown hair and his unbuttoned shirt flapping against his back, looking as if he had stepped right out of one of those Westerns he loved so much.

We knew precisely where Terry picked up that philosophy. It came from our Grandma Alice, my mom's mother. She preached to us all the time about life being a journey, about taking time to watch the scenery as it passed by, and not taking it for granted. She told us to enjoy the ride, even if there's a bump or a stumble, a breakdown or a big old mud hole along the way that discourages us from going on. It would all ultimately be worth our perseverance, she promised. God always makes sure of that.

In due course, I would have occasions when I would seriously question her sunny outlook on life. There would be times when I was certain that God had placed more on me than I could bear, when I couldn't fathom what His plan was for me. That's when I needed Terry or Grandma Alice or someone like them to remind me about life's journey and the obstacles we all encounter on the way and how those things that don't kill us serve to make us stronger.

I was the oldest of the five Blackburn children, and sometimes I felt more like I was their mother than their big sister. I was the one who had to fix whatever was broken for my siblings, doctoring skinned knees or helping to patch up broken hearts.

That's what hurt me so badly as the end neared for Terry. There was absolutely nothing I could do for my brother, nothing that would take away the pain, the awful certainty of imminent death. Neither from him nor from my own aching soul. And I felt as if the frustration of it all was going to kill me.

It seemed as if God had placed a huge obstacle in the trail before me. I saw no way around it.

But then my poor, sick brother did the most wonderful, loving thing for me. He gave me the chance to do one last good turn for him. He allowed me to give him the one thing he most wanted before he reached his life's final destination.

He asked me to go with him on one final Christmas ride together.

I'm convinced that Terry knew that short ride was exactly what it would take to heal my heartsickness, that it would help me see the reason for the other tragedies that had occurred in my own life's journey. It would give me new resolve even as it pointed me toward an exciting new fork in the road. And I'm convinced, too, that it also gave my brother hope in the midst of a hopeless situation.

He was right, of course, and I'm thankful to God

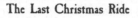
that I had the opportunity to be there with Terry on that final ride. My brother had had a remarkable passage through life, and he thoroughly enjoyed the scenery along the way. Short though it was, he managed to make the most of it.

In the end, he was able to show me a way to do the same, just as he had urged us all to do back when we were kids, riding our horses through the meadows and cedar glades around home.

Then, that done, Terry Blackburn spurred his horse one more time and rode away into the dusk.

1

IT WAS AN unseasonably warm day, about a week before Christmas Day, with a brilliant sun shining down, sparkling off the tinsel on the tree where it stood next to the window. I had made a tape of special seasonal songs I thought Terry would enjoy, many of them done by artists I had worked with in Nashville, and it was playing quietly through the speakers while I cleaned up the breakfast dishes.

I could see him struggling to move his arm enough to reach the control on his wheelchair. He had slumped over sideways and didn't have the strength to free his arm, and he was behaving as stubbornly as ever, insisting on doing as much for himself as he could. But he obviously was having trouble accomplishing even the simplest of tasks.

"Can I help you, Terry?" I asked as I walked toward him.

He looked at me quickly, glaring angrily at me with his dark brown eyes.

"No! I don't need you!" he snapped. The tone of his voice was cutting, bordering on vicious.

I stepped back, hurt. There had been plenty of examples of Terry's temper throughout the long ordeal, but he usually directed it at the wheelchair, the bedpan, or one of the dogs who got in the way of his progress toward the patio. This was the first time he had lashed out directly at me.

I bit my lip and tried not to let him see the tears in my eyes as I fled back to the kitchen and busied myself again with a skillet I was scouring.

He finally managed to get his arm free and the control activated. I watched out of the corner of my eye as he slowly made his way out the door and into the sunshine on the patio. I stepped to the window to make sure he had stopped before running off the edge, as he had almost done a couple of times.

As I tried to cool the hot coals of my hurt feelings, I reminded myself that as frustrating as Terry's condition was for the rest of us, it had to be unbearable for a vigorous, larger-than-life man as my brother to be in this hopeless, pain-ridden situation.

I watched him squirm and wiggle until he was sitting almost upright in the chair. He somehow managed to hold his head high, his chin jutted out as if he was defying his fate, and he stared off into the distance toward where his horses grazed and to where a thick growth of cedars had almost concealed the Indian mound we had played on when we were children.

He looked so frail and vulnerable sitting there in the December sun, but he seemed determined to sit up straight in the wheelchair. My heart broke for him.

Eventually I sucked up my pride, grabbed a jar

of his baby food, and went outside. I carefully eased myself down into one of the patio chairs near him. After a bit, I dipped a small spoonful of the food and fed it to him. He accepted the bland concoction silently. I continued spooning it into his mouth until it was all gone. He ate as if he was unaware of what he was doing and had not tasted a single bite of it.

He still had not acknowledged that I was there.

The sun was wonderfully warm, the air pleasant, fragrant with the smell of the cedars that grew all around Terry's place. The horses had noticed us sitting there in the sun and had ambled over to the fence nearest us as they foraged for any food they could find on the bare ground.

It was a while before I dared to speak. I was unsure if Terry had calmed down yet or if he might snarl at me again. I decided to take my chance.

"Terry, do you remember how we used to ride the horses across these hills until it was too dark to see where we were going? He remained silent but nodded slightly. "And remember how we were so busy playing that we would only head home when we heard Mother calling to tell us that supper was ready?"

He nodded again. His lips moved, and I strained to hear him.

"Supper was sure . . . sure better than . . . than that stuff," he growled and eyed the empty baby food jar that was still in my lap. I shrugged and grinned.

"Sure was. Remember how David used to punch those holes in his baseball cap and pull his curls through and make us all laugh?" He gave me a weak, crooked smile. "Or the time you got so mad 'cause we wouldn't let you drag that beautiful Christmas tree back to the woods and replant it?" He wrinkled his nose and shook his head slightly. "And remember why we named the horses what we did? David liked watching the sky from on top of the Indian mounds, so 'Spotted Cloud' it was. And I loved Roy Roger's horse, Trigger. But you? You had a crush on our Avon Lady, who just happened to be named Polly." His shoulders shook slightly, as if he may have been about to laugh. "Remember how we'd tie Polly, Spotted Cloud, and Trigger to a tree, and we'd get up on top of that Indian mound and lie down in the grass and talk about all our dreams and disappointments? And how we would lie there and plan out the rest of our lives?"

"Wasn't . . . much else . . . to do," Terry said, almost in an inaudible whisper.

"That's true. About the most exciting thing to do in Burnout was going down to the general store and watching Mr. Elliot slice bacon." Mr. Elliot owned our town's other grocery store as well as the local egg farm.

We watched the horses for a moment. Far off in the distance, a lone automobile made its way along the highway toward Burnout.

"Looks like you . . . you'll be . . . the only one of us . . . to live . . . those dreams we talked about."

It took him a long time to get the words out. I didn't answer. I didn't have a comment for that one. We were quiet for a while longer. Terry finally spoke again.

"I . . . miss . . . them."

"Who, honey?"

"David. Phillip. Grandma Alice."

"Yeah, I do, too, Terry. Every day I'm alive. But I plan on seeing them again someday."

I bit my tongue. I don't know what made me say those words. It wasn't something that should be spoken so bluntly to a dying man. As soon as the sentence was out of my mouth, I looked at him to see if I might have sparked another angry outburst. Instead, he was smiling as best he could with his halfway-paralyzed face. And his eyes fairly sparkled when he cut them toward me.

"Me, too. Me, too."

Then he was quiet again, watching the horses playing with each other in the pasture like high-spirited kids. When he spoke again, his voice was as strong as I had heard it in months.

"I hope I leave some tall, strong trees in my place," he said.

"What?"

"Like Grandma Alice said. That a strong, straight tree just makes room for lots more like it to grow in its place when it's gone."

23

"Yeah, I remember." Not a Christmas had gone by that we didn't reminisce about Terry and that old tree he wanted to save. As long as she was with us, our granny would just smile and wink at us every time the story was told.

Terry twisted around as much as he could manage so he could look at me face-to-face.

"Edith, can you do something for me?"

"Of course, dear. Anything."

"I want to take that Christmas ride you promised me. Remember? Before my surgery? And I want you to take it with me."

I wiped the tears out of my eyes with both hands and turned away, hoping he wouldn't see.

"Sure! Absolutely! When?"

"Right now."

Right now? But there was nobody there but my sister, Kim, and me. I thought he had meant later. Someday down the road that might not ever come. Someday when Mark, my husband, and my son, Linc, and Kim's husband would be there to help.

Not now! Please, Terry! Don't ask me to keep that promise now!

But instead of sitting there and telling him all the reasons why this couldn't happen, I jumped up, ran inside, and called for Kim. She looked at me as if I had taken leave of my senses when I told her what we were going to do.

"Sis, how in the world are we going to . . . ?" But she must have seen the determination in my face. "Well, let's get to it then."

I ran down to the gate and called over a couple of Terry's horses, put on their bridles, and led them to the barn to saddle them up. Kim helped Terry maneuver the wheelchair over the rough gravel and uneven ground between the house and the barn. We positioned his chair atop a small embankment and stood the horse next to him as close as we could get. Somehow, we got him to his feet, placed his left foot into the stirrup, and shoved him over onto the horse's back, then threw his other leg over the saddle.

Lord knows what would have happened if we had dropped him or if he had kept going right on over the horse. He would have landed hard. I don't know if both of us could have gotten him up off the ground and back into the chair. Or if he had taken a tumble off the horse while he was riding, he could have been hurt badly. For some reason, none of that seemed to enter our minds at the time. We just knew we had to get him up on the mount and allow him to ride. There was no option.

I climbed up on my own horse and moved over next to Terry to take the reins of his steed. I figured I would lead him a few steps around the barnyard and end the ride before something horrible happened.

"Hand the reins to me, Edith," he said. I did as I was told.

Slowly, deliberately, he nudged the flanks of his horse with his thighs, and she stepped away from the embankment. I don't know how he did it, but Terry sat up straight and tall in the saddle, as if there was not a thing in the world wrong with him.

Kim had had the foresight to bring her camera, and she snapped away. Those pictures today show my brother sitting ramrod straight, the reins held high in his hands, the warm breeze blowing his gapped hair, and him with a pronounced but uneven grin on his wan face. I can only imagine the effort and willpower it took for him to keep himself upright in the saddle, to hold onto those reins as we walked the horses slowly around the backyard of his home.

For a moment, I was afraid he might suddenly kick the horse into a gallop, that maybe he would try to trot her out into the pasture and head off toward the Indian mound. But Terry knew better. He didn't want to put his sisters through any more trauma than he already had. In just a few short moments, he began to slump, his strength clearly sapped by the effort of his ride.

I took the reins and led the horse back over to the embankment. We carefully slid our brother off and sat him back down into the wheelchair.

Then—right there in the barnyard with the horses watching—all three hugged and cried and hugged some more.

"Thank you, Edith, Kim," he croaked. "Just

knowing I might one day get to ride that horse again gave me hope when it looked like I had no hope left." He reached for enough breath to finish what he wanted to say. We waited patiently. "I knew you would keep your promise, Edith. You'll never know what this Christmas ride meant to me."

Or to me, brother. Or to me.

2

THE SIGN BESIDE the narrow rural blacktop highway read "Burnout, Alabama. Population 679," but somebody had taken a dollop of red clay mud and added the word "Plum" above the community's name. They had also smeared a "t" in the middle of it, so it now proclaimed this little burgh to be "Burnt Plum Out."

"That's terrible," my mother scoffed as we drove past on our way home from shopping for school clothes in Russellville. "Some kids have defaced that sign again. They ought to be ashamed. I'm sure their momma is embarrassed as she can be, the poor thing!"

It was all we could do to suppress our sniggers as my brothers and I tried not to look at each other. Eye contact would have been more than any of us could stand. My three younger brothers and I knew only too well who those kids were. What we didn't anticipate—and we certainly should have by then—was just how fastidious our mother was.

Mother was a beautiful woman, with sandy brown hair and spring-leaf-green eyes, a good mom, a regionally renowned cook. She was fastidious about her appearance and loved creams on her face, and she would regularly go to a beauty shop in Halltown and tell Miss Jane that she wanted "the works."

But as my Grandma Alice always reminded us, Mother had been sickly since she was a little girl. She was afflicted with "bad nerves." Sometimes her headaches or a clutching wave of depression would send her off to her bedroom where she would take the better part of a week to recuperate in the cool, quiet darkness she found there. The curtains were drawn to blot out any hint of daylight and we knew instinctively not to make any noise while she "got better."

Daddy was a good man as well, although he always seemed to be off working somewhere. He was handsome, blessed with soot-black hair, brown eyes, and muscles that confirmed that he was an extremely hard worker, sometimes holding down three jobs at once. He owned a country grocery store and a fleet of delivery trucks, yet he still held down a full time job as the head mechanic for the Tennessee Valley Authority works in Muscle Shoals. He told us he worked hard because he wanted to make certain that we grew up with more than he ever had. That meant the biggest, newest car, the nicest school clothes, and the only brick house (and the only one with two inside bathrooms) in all of Burnout. But it also meant that he was up and gone to work before we ever crawled out of bed for school in the morning. And when we turned in for the night, he often was still at work or off on a run in one of his trucks.

We may have had new cars, fashionable clothes,

and two inside bathrooms, but I don't remember ever taking a family vacation together.

Mother's bouts of depression and Daddy's absence settled my fate. As Grandma Alice told me, since I was the oldest and Mother was the way she was, and our daddy was such a hard worker and away most of the time, I would have to be both sister and mother to the boys, and to baby sister Kim when she came along much later. That also meant I had to keep the house spotless. Mother would not tolerate dirt or disorder, whether she was physically able to clean and straighten herself or not. That was just the way it was in our family, and I had to accept my lot.

So it should not have surprised us when Mother proclaimed that there was no way she was going to allow that dirty, defaced sign to remain visible. "Why, anybody could pass by and see it and think less of those of us who lived in our little community." As we pulled up the long driveway to our house, Mother began barking out our marching orders.

"Edith, you go in there and get me the Spic-and-Span and the mop bucket full of hot water. Get that water as hot as you can stand it. Boys, y'all get the packages into the house and then fetch me some rags from out of the garage. We're going to clean up that sign before somebody passes by and gets a look at that mess. They'll think we are all a bunch of hicks around here."

"But Momma . . ."

"Hush! Be quick. I feel a headache coming on. We got to get back so Edith can have supper ready for Daddy when he gets home from work."

Cleaning up signs we had mischievously defaced ourselves was not how we had planned to pass the rest of that precious late-summer afternoon. The first day of school loomed ahead, promising to bring an abrupt end to what had been a glorious summer so far. Darkness was already chopping off the ends of our days before we were ready to give them up, and we had much better use for dwindling daylight than cleaning up our red-clay mischief or cooking supper.

We had balked in the first place at the shopping trip to Russellville, usually a fun journey, with candy bars and jawbreakers and cold bottles of orange soda pop our reward for not fighting. But not on such a glorious day as this. Not with so much playing to be done before the oak leaves went orange and yellow and the school bell rang again.

Mother ignored our protests except to tell us why the trip was essential.

"The way you are all growing, you'll have to try on everything to make sure it fits. It's too far to drive all the way back up there to take things back and swap them for something that fits."

We still did not understand. Didn't she know that we should have been in full-play mode, aboard our three horses, galloping across the fields and pastures that stretched out invitingly from our place? We should have been planning strategy beneath the fragrant pines, creating immense, sweeping fantasies that involved cowboys and Indians, knights and warriors, banditos and Texas Rangers, and imaginary guest appearances by Roy Rogers and Dale Evans, Gene Autry, and Zorro.

We Blackburn children had all been blessed with fertile imaginations, and we put them to good use as we created and acted out our dramas, making up characters and plot as we went. We explored new worlds and won vicious, pitched battles against imaginary enemies charging toward us over the gently rolling hills past stately cedars and tall, spindly pines.

As the big sister, I came up with most of the scenarios that we acted out, but my brothers happily went along with them, embellishing their parts mightily with their vivid thoughts. They usually emerged the heroes as they overcame daunting odds, rescued the damsel in distress (me), and rode away victoriously into a spectacular sunset.

The endings were always happy in our play world. The heroes were invincible.

There were usually the three of us—David, Terry, and I—and then Phillip came along. Our sister, Kim, was a late arrival and missed most of the fun.

David, my oldest brother, was only a year younger than I. He liked to be Tex Ritter, Rex Allen, the Lone Ranger, or Gene Autry. Those were his favorites from the afternoon TV shows we watched when a thunderstorm or freezing rain chased us inside. When he wasn't firing away at bad hombres with his BB gun, he sat on his horse plunking his guitar, singing cowboy songs, and yodeling to the cows, just like his favorite singing cowboys. The cows paid him no mind, but he didn't care.

I typically was Dale Evans or Annie Oakley, singing my own western sonnets while we searched the pasture for rustlers or train robbers or invading aliens from Mars. Sometimes my brothers would shoot their BB guns at me or at my horse. They would get spankings from Momma when I tattled on them. I suppose they figured it was worth the whippings, because they'd do it all over again when they had the chance.

It was an idyllic time. Our summer days were filled with playing and riding and playing some more. We were so involved in our elaborate play-acting that we often didn't notice the sticky Alabama heat or the rumble of approaching thunderstorms. The lightning and wind and rain would be upon us before we were aware of them, and we had to ride back through the deluge to the barn. We usually were soaked to the skin by the time we got there, but we continued our adventures in the big hayloft in the barn until it got too dark to see anymore. Another favorite refuge from storms was the old storage building behind the house. It was actually the back end of an old peddler's truck that once had been used to make deliveries to country folk. When that came to an end, Daddy bought it for storage, but we quickly turned it into our own playhouse.

When the storms didn't stop us, we played until we were too tired to go on. Then, once each day's story wound down and our mission was accomplished, the darkness threatened to close in on us as we lay atop one of the three Indian mounds in the pasture. There always seemed to be a cool breeze atop them, and they offered just enough altitude to prolong the sunlight a few minutes longer, too. Anything to stretch the day! From up there we could also keep a wary eye out for approaching renegades or rustlers that might have eluded our posse that day.

Or we'd spy a regiment of Napoleon's army trying to get the jump on us.

Sometimes, in the hottest part of summer, we preferred ending our day of play on Goat Bluff, an outcropping of rocks that overlooked the creek at one of its widest, deepest points. It was a wonderful swimming hole. The ten-foot cliff was a perfect place from which to dive right into the cold, spring-fed water. It was an absolute antidote to the fatigue, sweat, and dust of the day. A rope swing had been tied to an overhanging elm, too, and if we timed our run and our swing out over the creek just right, we could land right over the spot where the cold spring water bubbled up from the rocks on the bottom of the creek. The water was so cold it took our breath away, but it was refreshing to our tired bodies and waning spirits.

We called that swimming spot the "blue hole."

After a good, refreshing swim, we climbed the Indian mound and lay in the grass, allowing the warm breeze and the last of the day's sunshine to dry us.

The horses—Polly, Spotted Cloud, and Trigger—were tied off, grazing peacefully. We were refreshed from the swim or from lying there on our backs in the shaded green grass, and we were finally still for a few minutes. We became quiet as we watched the cloud formations overhead or the first of the evening's fireflies winking at us from the filmy-pink mimosa trees at the far end of the pasture.

That's when we finally got serious. We would talk about our dreams and wishes and frustrations until it eventually got dusky dark and we knew we had to end the day.

"I'm going to be a movie star and a singer, like Dale Evans," I usually announced.

At any other place or time, such a pronouncement would earn me laughter, catcalls, and ridicule. Not there. Not on top of that mound with the crickets just beginning their nightly concert and the horses snorting softly at the foot of the mound.

It seemed to be the one place where we could open up and share our deepest thoughts, where we could speak of the tough moments between Mom and Dad. There we could reveal our innermost dreams and fears to each other, where they were safe, never to be repeated elsewhere, not even in the most heated argument when they might have supplied the perfect get-even barb to hurl.

Once spoken out loud atop that Indian mound, those thoughts were sacred.

"I am going to breed racehorses and own a cattle farm," David would declare. "And build race cars so I can ride as fast as I can go. And I'm going to win the Charlotte race."

That was a natural. Dad's hobby was rebuilding old cars. He kept a '56 Chevy he had souped up in the barn, and all of us—all except Mother, that is—went with him when he took it to the drag strip a few times in Haleyville to compete.

David was tall and lean, blessed with deep brown eyes and the most amazing shock of curly blonde hair. Since he was already so tall, it was obvious he would have a hard time fitting into a racecar, at least to me and his younger brothers. None of us ever challenged his dream, and we just chewed on pine needles and watched the clouds above us change first to pink and then to blood red.

David had a wonderful sense of humor. To make us laugh, he'd cut holes in an old baseball cap and pull the sandy ringlets through like curly spikes sticking out all over his head. David loved life and tried to make certain everyone around him did, too. He found humor in almost everything.

He loved to tease us, his big brown eyes twinkling when he inevitably got a rise out of us. Nobody could stay mad at him long, though.

David was a natural comedian, a gifted mimic, and as we lay on top of the mound, he would often keep a running commentary going about each car or truck that passed by on the highway below us. Sometimes he pretended to be the rock-and-roll disk jockeys we heard on the radio, introducing the records they spun. Or he was a sportscaster, describing the action of the Alabama Crimson Tide as they defeated another opponent under the legendary Bear Bryant.

David especially enjoyed it when Mrs. Magoo

drove past in her long, overloaded station wagon, blue smoke pouring out from behind and all four fenders flapping and rattling like some fat bird trying to take off. She was the wife of the man who owned the lumber mill in Burnout, and she drove like a man, with her elbow out the window and a big, thick cigar stuck in her mouth. The rest of her old Plymouth wagon was overflowing with her eight or nine kids—we were never certain of exactly how many she had—hanging out the windows on both sides and at the rear of the car. David suggested that the kids might be trying to escape their momma's cigar smoke. Or maybe get away from each other. Those kids were fixtures in Burnout, wrestling in the dirt in front of our father's store and fighting with each other or anyone else they could engage. The amazing thing was that none of them seemed to be over ten years of age.

"And heeerrre they come around the first turn!" David would announce, using a pinecone for a microphone and dragging out the word "here" in a perfect nasally imitation of the announcer's call of the Kentucky Derby on the radio. "It's Mrs. Magoo leading the pack as they approach the home stretch. How many kids does she have aboard this trip? I'd say a couple of dozen . . . maybe three or four more than last week. Twins? Triplets? Quadruplets? Who knows? Where do they all come from, ladies and gentlemen? Does she grow 'em like melons in Arlander's watermelon patch?"

David kept the description going until the car was long gone, leaving only a lingering cloud of blue smoke. By then we were giggling, rolling around in the fragrant grass and ignoring the big-eyed, curious stares of the horses.

I was closer to David than I was to the other boys, likely because we were not only closest in age but we were also kindred spirits. We seemed to know what the other was thinking and shared the mutual admiration that only very close siblings seem to be able to manage. He was so intelligent but with a stellar wit that never failed to make me laugh out loud, even when I most wanted to cry. And he did it often, because it was his often-voiced opinion that I was much too serious for my own good.

"I want to be an architect," Terry declared. Some of us weren't sure what an architect actually was, but if Terry wanted to be one, none of us doubted he would be. "I want to build houses and buildings. Even bigger ones than they got up in Florence. Maybe build dams, too, like Joe Wheeler or Bear Creek. Why not? Yeah, I want to build dams and bridges and I want to build highways that run all the way to St. Louis."

Terry was third in age on the Blackburn stair steps, three years younger than David. He, too, had brown eyes, but his hair was much darker than the rest of our blonde manes, more like Daddy's. He liked to wear his locks long, down the back of his neck, and from the time he was a little kid, he always carried a comb with him, to make certain his hair was perfectly groomed. When it got especially long, Mother would fuss and tell him he had to get a haircut. So would Daddy, if he was home long enough to notice. Terry became very adept at stonewalling, putting off the shearing as long as he possibly could.

"You know what happened to Samson when he got his hair cut," he would remind us, a serious look on his face. It seemed he paid attention in Sunday school when it served his purpose. But inevitably, Daddy took the boys to the garage and made them sit on a bar stool for a haircutting. He had an expression on his face like a mad scientist as he sheared away all that hair, giving each brother a GI cut to last several months.

That's when Terry would wear a baseball cap until it grew back out long enough for him to part and comb it just right.

Terry was tall like David, but he was much stockier. Also like his big brother, he was very athletic from the time he learned to walk. He could knock a squirrel off a tree limb with a rock from thirty feet. He was also the most determined person I have ever known. When he was fourteen, I watched him work all day to untangle fishing line from an old rod and reel he was trying to salvage.

"Terry, that thing's old and the line's probably rotten anyway," I pointed out to him. "Why don't you just throw it away and use one of the good rods if you want to fish?"

He looked at me as if I had taken leave of my senses.

"Nothing wrong with this one," he answered with his crooked grin. "Besides, I started to get it untangled and I'm not going to quit until I finish the job."

And that was that.

Terry was also the only one among us with a quick temper. That made him an easy target for David, who loved to "get his goat" with his pranks and kidding. But then, after lighting his fuse and getting the desired explosion, he'd have Terry laughing again in no time.

There was one other thing about our dark-haired middle brother. He was the take-charge one, even though he was third oldest among us. If there was a task to be done, he saw it through to completion. He drew out the plan in the dirt, assigned tasks,

46

then saw it completed, even if he ended up having to do the bulk of the work himself. Later, when he was grown, he was the one drafted to lead the building committee at church or to ramrod the community projects at the Masonic lodge. If Terry Blackburn was involved, things got done, and they got done right.

Sometimes, when we were resting on the Indian mound, he would disappear and we wouldn't know where he had gone. Then he'd come galloping back in a few minutes with a big watermelon he had picked—without bothering to ask, of course—from our Uncle Arlander's watermelon patch. We'd put it in the creek so it'd be nice and cold by the time we got ready for it. Then we'd bust it open on a big rock and eat it. We liked the sweet yellow ones best. Many times, that watermelon made up our lunch, since riding back to the house and fixing ourselves sandwiches interrupted the storyline of whatever adventure we were playing out that day.

When I close my eyes today, I can still see Terry clearly as a young, robust man—six-foot-one, strong, very good looking, a guy who took pride not only in how he looked but also in everything else about his life. He rivaled Mother when it came to being fastidious. He would not tolerate messes. He was full of spit and vinegar, too, but everyone enjoyed being around him, especially the girls. But it seemed he always left them wanting more from him than he was willing to give. When we all grew older, I thought of him as a man made of iron but with a soft, warm heart. I assumed he could build or fix anything, and he never disappointed me. His determination and attention to detail was an inspiration to my brothers, our little sister, and me. Everyone he met admired his persistence and work ethic.

Phillip was the youngest of the brothers. He came to our adventures late, just before we gave them up for sports, school, cars, and romance. He was the quiet one of the bunch, another handsome, brown-eyed, blonde-haired Blackburn. He laughed and played, just as we did, and quickly became a role-player in the fantasyland we maintained for our own amusement out there in the back pasture. But there was always a deep sadness in his eyes, as if there was some melancholy there that none of the rest of us shared.

"I am going to be a songwriter," he announced one day as we sprawled around on top of the Indian mound. "I'm going to be like our Uncle Harty, Shorty, and Anthony Hacker. I'll have a band like them, and we'll play all over the state. Up in Tennessee, too. Shoot, we'll be on the Grand Ole Opry!"

The rest of us looked at each other. It would have broken the code if we had scoffed at his dream, but we couldn't figure why our baby brother wanted to emulate Mom's brothers. Their singing and songwriting had brought great pleasure but also great sadness to the family. It had led to their heavy drinking and notorious lifestyle.

"A songwriter?" I finally asked. "Why?"

"I just think it would be the most wonderful thing in the world if I could make up a song that would cause people to cry."

We remained silent for a bit, contemplating Phillip's ambition.

Then we were busy, laughing, finding animal

shapes in the clouds, waiting for Mrs. Magoo to drive past in her old station wagon loaded with her ragamuffins.

We didn't give Phillip's dream any more thought.

We almost lost Terry when he was twelve. It was a foreshadowing of the tragedies that seemed to gang up on us later in our lives.

It was a hot summer evening that followed another hot day of playing in the fields. We had a baseball game to go to. I always drove to the games, the boys riding with me, and tonight was supposed to be no different. However, for some reason Terry wanted to ride his motor scooter instead, and Mom finally gave in and agreed, but only if I followed along right behind him in the car with David and Phillip.

It was a great night. We won the baseball game in front of a big home crowd. Our cousin Roger and our Uncle Larry were the heroes, getting key hits late in the game. Some of my friends wanted me to go with them to listen to a local band rehearsal afterwards, and David said it would be okay. He reminded me that he was fourteen, after all, and could drive home with Phillip and follow along behind Terry on his little motor scooter. David drove all the time, and I had no doubt that all of my brothers would be fine. But I had promised Mother that I would follow Terry home myself, and I was torn, but finally I gave into the excitement of being with my friends, dancing, listening to music, and having fun for a change instead of playing momma for my brothers.

As David, Terry, and Phillip were heading across the Red Bay Bottoms, a carload of drunks came barreling up behind David and Phillip, then swerved around them and back in front of the car. They must not have seen Terry on his motor scooter.

The impact sent the little bike and its rider high into the air. Terry landed in a ditch beside his scooter, his body limp. There was blood everywhere.

Soon the state trooper, an ambulance, and a flock of people returning from the baseball game were there. Terry was rushed to the little hospital in Red Bay where my aunt Linda Blackburn was the head emergency room nurse. A family friend came to find me, and another went to get my mom and dad at home.

The scene at the hospital was a terrible one. There was a lot of crying, guilt, and confusion. It did not look good for Terry. He had a severe head injury and was unconscious. The decision was made to rush him to the hospital in Florence where there was a neurosurgeon and better equipment. Aunt Linda climbed into the ambulance and rode alongside Terry, clocking his pulse and counting his respirations all the way. Mom, Dad, David, Phillip, and I rode with Uncle Raymond, Aunt Linda's husband and my dad's brother.

It was the longest, most horrible ride of my life. Mother alternately sobbed and screamed at me, "It's your fault!" I was already wracked with guilt over my bad decision in sending the boys home alone, and Mother's words stung like bees.

Terry survived the delicate operation in Florence that night, but he was unconscious for a month, his brain swelling, teetering on the brink of death the entire time. Mother and Daddy sat up with him at the hospital the first day. Then Daddy had to go back to driving one of his trucks. Mother stayed the entire month. She said she wouldn't leave until Terry did.

I remember lying in the bed at Grandma Blackburn's house where I slept each night alongside Phillip and David. Our sister Kim was only two at the time and she was with Mom's sister, Lela Myrick. I could not sleep. I wished I could be there with Terry, taking care of him. But I was charged with caring for the other boys. I remember ironing their Sunday suits, just in case there was to be a funeral, my tears falling on the fabric as I worked. I couldn't stand the thought of Terry finally waking up one day and not being there with him. I fussed until Grandma Blackburn assured me she or Grandpa or Uncle Larry would take me to see him the next day.

Still, I tried to stifle my crying so I wouldn't wake my brothers. I was so afraid that I would never see Terry alive again, never see him astride his horse galloping in our direction with one of those big watermelons curled in his arms while he held onto

the horse with his knees, his long hair tossed by the wind.

I had horrible dreams, too. Dreams that God might come take one of my other brothers away from me. That would be my fault, too. I felt so guilty, so scared.

I wondered if my bad decision had caused Terry's accident. Was it my fault that my brother was lying in the hospital near death? Would this accident have happened even if *I* had been the one driving behind Terry instead of David, or could I have stopped it somehow if I had been where I was supposed to be?

As it turned out, Terry was too stubborn to die. Even though he was unconscious for a month, he pulled through, soon bragging about being tougher than some dadgum old Chevrolet full of drunks. There was only a limp and a scar or two to show for all he went through that long summer. He never complained about the pain or the crutches or the double vision or the loss of taste.

He first noticed he was regaining his sense of

taste when he took a swallow of a soft drink I had poured into a dark glass for him.

"Edith, this is a Mountain Dew!" he declared.

I cried with joy at those simple words.

He learned to crawl and then to walk again before it was even time to go back to school in the fall. During the summer, he chomped at the bit and talked about how he couldn't wait to get back up on Polly and ride around the pasture again.

But it was not that easy.

When Terry came home from the hospital, it was a tough time for him, and for the rest of us, too. The boy who always had won the races with his brothers and sister had to crawl across the floor like a baby, struggling to go even a short distance. His athletic career was over, too, but he never complained.

Still, that experience helped make Terry the kind of man he became. He was the one who took on the impossible and somehow managed to get it accomplished, no matter the odds. He also was a practical, no-nonsense man, not sentimental at all;

and even when he did something kind and gener-
ous for someone, when anyone tried to thank him,
he would wave off the gratitude as if praise was
insulting.

Terry's would ultimately be the hardest ride of
all. And he would be the one who would teach me
some of life's most valuable lessons on courage.

3

MUSIC WAS AN important part of our lives while we were growing up. It seemed music was in our genetic makeup, passed down from generation to generation, as it was to so many others who grew up in the South. We were second cousins to Elvis Presley, but there were plenty of other less-famous, musically talented folks on both sides of our family as far back as we could trace. Some of them preferred singing to talking.

Each of us Blackburn kids gravitated toward his

or her favorite instrument. Terry played the drums.
Phillip and David chose the guitar. I played piano
and sang. Sometimes when it rained or was too cold
to be outside, we'd leave the horses in the barn, pull
out our instruments, gather in the big living room,
and play and sing together for hours. We first mim-
icked the country stars we heard on the Grand Ole
Opry broadcasts. When he got home in time on Sat-
urdays, Daddy liked to listen to the radio show as it
beamed in from Nashville, and we would stay awake
as long as we could and listen, too.

Later, we either did our own renditions of
hymns or gospel songs or performed country and
even rock 'n' roll songs we'd heard on the radio. We
also did songs from the variety shows we watched on
television or at the picture show and drive-in movies
we sometimes attended in Red Bay or Russellville or
Florence.

If they heard us doing rock 'n' roll, Mother or
Daddy would fuss.

"Ya'll don't be doing that kind of song! It's sinful,
with all that yelling and those drums."

It was hard for them to maintain that stance when we watched our cousin Elvis as he appeared for the first time on *The Ed Sullivan Show*. There he was—or at least him from the waist up—right there on the TV. How could that be wrong? He was part of our family, after all.

Still, we mostly preferred country and gospel songs. We played "Hound Dog" or "Don't Be Cruel" to see if we could get a rise out of our parents.

Music was also a big part of our family gatherings, especially on holidays. Grandpa Walter Hacker held a huge get-together each year on the Fourth of July. He hauled in a truckload of watermelons on one of his logging trucks and spread them out under a big shade tree in front of their house on Hacker Road. He arranged pork shoulders on old metal grates he collected and kept a fire under them until they were smoked and succulent, watching over them all day. Grandma Alice was there, too, her apron wrapped around her and a small mop in her hand to smooth on the homemade barbecue sauce. Meanwhile Aunt Jackie and

Aunt Lela and Varnese had a big, black pot of stew simmering. Everyone who came brought potato salad, vegetables, and desserts, as well as their crank-type ice cream freezers. Someone would make a run to the ice plant in Muscle Shoals, and by mid-afternoon everyone with a good arm was cranking away on one of those freezers. We usually even had catfish caught fresh from Grandpa Hacker's lake. It was one huge feast!

The guitars, banjos, harmonicas, and fiddles came out, too. I suspect there were a few whiskey bottles hidden in those cases as well, but no one ever said anything about that. Everyone arranged chairs and blankets around the sprawling front yard amid my grandmother's beautiful flowers.

The jam session lasted until the last visitor packed up and went home that night. Grandpa's house had a big, wide front porch that circled around three-quarters of the structure. That served as our stage. As soon as one bunch finished a song, the next group would launch into another one, though everyone usually plucked along in the background, chording along with whatever was being played.

Sometimes several hundred folks showed up at Grandpa's Independence Day affair, most of them kin to each other. It was heady stuff to have that many people listening to the music we made, to hear their shouts and applause when we finished our songs. Our cousin Elvis even entertained there one year before he was discovered in Memphis.

My brothers and I set up near the steps so we could keep an eye on the ice cream freezers and gauge their progress even as we picked and sang. Eating home-cranked ice cream was about the only thing we preferred to playing and singing.

Grandma Alice made certain someone pulled her old upright piano out of the parlor onto the porch for me to play. We always got to do four or five songs, including mixing in "Hound Dog" among the gospel standards if we thought we could get away with it.

But we were always the first to break and run when the first freezer was opened to check the consistency of the ice cream. We wanted to be the first ones there with bowl and spoon to sample it and to claim the paddles from inside the freezer.

Independence Day always ended with fireworks and a few more songs on the porch.

Sometimes Mother's brothers and sisters would come over to our house for a visit and, it seemed, they often forgot to go back home. Long after Daddy and my brothers and I had gone to bed, they would still be up talking, laughing, and drinking coffee. That's when Mother would tiptoe into my room and awaken me.

"Edith, get up and come in here and play the piano for everybody."

"Aw, Mother. I'm sleepy and in the morning we have to . . ."

"Come on, now. Just one or two sacred songs. Do "Amazing Grace" and "Peace in the Valley" for us. That's all. And maybe one of Jimmy Dean's recitations. Then you can go on back to bed."

Mother was usually the one who insisted we get to bed early so we would be sharp for school the next day. That rule went out the window when her family was visiting us and she was ready to show me off to them.

I would dutifully traipse into the living room and play for them. The "few songs" turned into a full-blown concert, complete with requests from the crowd. I ended up playing for hours, my fingers sore and my eyelids so heavy I could hardly see the sheet music in front of me, let alone my math book the next day in school.

But secretly, I loved it. Loved the attention, the applause, the smiles on their faces as they watched me, nodding their heads in time to the music I made.

That feeling would never go away, and that family adulation fanned the embers of my Indian mound fantasy until it was a white-hot blaze.

4

As BIG AS our grandfather's Fourth of July celebration was, Christmas was our family's biggest holiday by far. The holiday season actually began for us before Thanksgiving and wasn't over until the day after the New Year. We started planning when the leaves first began to turn in October, and my brothers and I put together an elaborate musical production and played and sang holiday songs for our relatives and friends who came to visit. We worked for hours, selecting just the right songs to add to our repertoire for that year.

Then we rehearsed until we were hoarse to have it perfect for everyone who came and was forced to listen.

Mother's decorations for our hearth and mantle were exquisite for a country setting. I remember the garland with lots of candles and baby Jesus in a manger with Joseph and Mary placed on a white bearskin rug near the hearth. We always had a live Christmas tree in the den, and for more formal occasions, Mother had us put up her favorite silver tree with the wheel of colored lights bouncing off it in the living room. We were allowed to go in the den when we had our nicest clothes on.

It was a special time at church, too. Some of us took part in the annual cantata, but we also were up front each Sunday morning and Wednesday night singing the carols by ourselves or joining in with the choir. We knew we were the stars of the show, and we relished our role.

All families have their own special holiday traditions, but the Blackburns had one that was uniquely our own. The day after Thanksgiving, we kids would get the horses out of the barn, saddle up, and ride out to the pasture, no matter how good or bad the weather might be. When Phillip was old enough, he doubled up with Terry, and when Kim came along, she rode with me. There was no all-day playing on these rides, no tilting with invading knights or fending off sneaky bushwhackers. No, we had serious business to attend to on our "Christmas ride."

I can't remember the first year we did it, but the ritual was the same each year. We rode around the pasture, taking our task to heart and looking for the fullest, prettiest cedar tree that we could find. We refused to accept the first one we saw. Each was carefully studied for size, fullness, and how straight the trunk stood. Then, when we all agreed on a particular cedar, we sawed down the tree and snaked it back to the house behind one of the horses.

Of course, we'd sing carols all the way to the tree and back and make a big deal of presenting it to Daddy and Mother. There was always hot chocolate and homemade fruitcake and Christmas-tree-shaped cookies waiting for us when we got back, even if I had to prepare them before we left.

Getting the tree stood up perfectly in its stand in the big front room took hours. Then we hung it full of the ornaments that had been handed down in our family for generations. And even then the singing would continue.

The ride took place every year until we headed off to our lives away from home, but we refused to allow the tradition to die. Even after most of us had moved away, we usually came back home at Thanksgiving each year, no matter where we happened to be or how topsy-turvy our lives had become, just so we could saddle the horses and ride out together to get the tree.

So much changed in our family as the years passed, but this was one thing we didn't want to let go. We no longer had summer adventures, and so we seemed especially desperate to cling to this one sacred Blackburn tradition.

On one special holiday we woke up the day after Thanksgiving to find a rare dusting of snow on the ground. We were all amazed! Grandpa Walter called it "hog killin' weather," the first cold snap of the season. It always seemed to hit about Thanksgiving, but it rarely brought real, honest-to-goodness snow. This was about as close to a white Christmas as we were likely to have in our part of the world.

Mother suggested we wait a couple of days to go get the tree, until the weather moderated. She was always afraid one of us would come down with pneumonia. We knew we couldn't break the tradition, not even by a couple of days. So, despite the flurries and the bitter wind, we saddled up the horses and rode out into the pasture anyway. We were in a hurry to get the job done before one of us froze to the saddle.

It took us longer than usual to locate the perfect tree that year. David found a nice, tall one, but the trunk forked and its backside was thin. I spotted what I was sure was a good one, but just before Terry put the saw to the trunk, he noticed a bird's nest in its branches, filled with blue bits of broken shell. He pulled away the saw and headed back to his horse.

"It's okay," David assured him, holding his mittens to his nose to try to keep it from freezing and

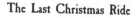

falling off. "That old momma bird is long gone to Florida by now. She won't care."

"No, she'll be back in the spring, and she'll look for that nest." Terry was only seven or eight that year, but he had already developed his rock-solid determination. When he said something, he meant it, and there was little point in arguing. "We shouldn't bother it. Besides, we can find a better Christmas tree than that old thing if we look just a little bit longer."

David made a silly face, imitating Terry's serious expression. David looked especially funny with his red nose and his eyes tearing in the bitter wind. I laughed, but Terry was already aboard his horse and was riding off, searching once more for the perfect Christmas tree.

A half hour later, we finally found what David and I agreed was a pretty good tree—tall, straight, full, and with no bird nest. Even if it wasn't ideal, it was too cold and the wind too biting for us to look any longer. If we didn't hurry, Christmas would be over even before we got back with a tree! We were all thinking of how good hot chocolate, a fire in the fireplace, and leftover Thanksgiving pumpkin pie would taste and had even stopped singing because the icy wind seemed to jerk our words out of the air and throw them out of earshot.

When we turned to look for Terry to tell him to bring the saw, we relized that he wasn't there and had pulled another of his disappearing acts. The wind was whipping little bits of hominy snow now, and it was downright cold out there in the pasture.

Then we heard him yelling at us from over near the creek.

"Come here! It's the best tree ever!"

David made circles at his temples with his fingers, signifying that our little brother was plumb goofy. We mounted back up and rode over to where he was waiting, leaving behind a perfectly good Christmas tree. But when we got there, we saw that, sure enough, our goofy little brother had located an absolutely beautiful cedar tree. It just might have been the best ever, exactly as he had declared.

Everyone who saw it over the next month said so, too. Its limbs were thick and dark green, its trunk tall and straight, and it proudly held an amazing number of ornaments and tinsel and angel hair and the big star on top, all without drooping one bit. There was no doubt that all the presents and anything Santa might bring would easily fit under its broad canopy, too. And it smelled so good! It filled the whole house with the fresh aroma of cedar, to us, the smell of Christmas.

We believed it was bad luck to take down the tree before New Year's Day, and so the day after New Year's Mother told us to drag our perfect Christmas tree outside before it caught fire or dropped every one of its needles on the parlor floor. David and I intended to pull it up into the edge of the woods and let it rot, but Terry pitched one of his famous fits. Stomping his foot and waving his finger at us, he vowed he was going to take it back to where we found it. He wanted to plant it in the ground so it would grow once more, so we could go back out there next year, pull it up, and use it again.

"It's too beautiful a tree to just let it die," he said, fighting back tears.

David and I were unable to reason with him, and the more we laughed and made fun of his silly idea, the madder he got. Grandma Alice Hacker finally stepped in with her unique wisdom to defuse the situation. She had been in the kitchen helping Mother and must have heard the commotion in the back yard.

"Terry, you are right, darlin'. That was . . . is . . . a very special Christmas tree. Maybe the best one I've ever seen, and the Lord's been good enough to let me see lots of them." Terry was still so mad he was red-faced and squint-eyed. His fists were balled at his sides, ready to fight for the life of his tree. "But when a tree that big and pretty and strong is cut down, you know what happens? It makes room for other trees to take root and grow in its place. It makes way for the sun and rain to get to the young trees. If you go back out there next year and find the spot where you got this tree, I bet you'll find five or six little cedars growing in that very same spot, on the way to being big, beautiful Christmas trees, just like this one. And since they came from the seed and roots of this tree, they'll grow tall and straight and strong, too, just like their daddy. Maybe grow up even better than this one did." Terry visibly calmed down a little, and Grandma Alice put her hand on his shoulder. "It's the same way with people, you know. If we grow strong and straight and give a good example for others to follow, we'll make room in the sunshine for lots of folks to do the same when we're gone. Especially them that have the same seed and roots as we do."

Whether he was only seven or eight years old or not, his grandmother's logic seemed to make perfectly good sense to Terry. He unclenched his fists and grabbed hold of the trunk of that tree he had so proudly chosen and started off to the woods, dragging what was left of it along behind him and leaving a trail of dead needles in its wake.

He still demanded that we have a funeral for it and that David play his guitar while we all sang "Oh, Christmas Tree" over its browning carcass.

I don't think any of us ever forgot Grandma Alice's words that day.

I know for a fact that my brother Terry never did.

5

OUR SISTER KIMBERLY came along much later, a late surprise for all of us. Things had not been going well between our parents, so we were surprised when we learned there was to be another little Blackburn soon. She would be fifteen years younger than I was. That meant she was too late to take part in our fantasy horseback adventures or our dream sessions out on the Indian mounds or our diving into the cold water off Goat Bluff. She was a beauty with big brown eyes, a fetching smile, and long legs.

Things had changed. I had moved on to high school. I had not given up on my Indian mound dreams of a career in show business, but I was also occupied with my after-school jobs and trying to get certain boys to notice me in study hall. I was especially interested in a tall fellow senior. One of my teachers, Barbara Cashion, had been trying to get us together since our junior year. He was Mark Aldridge, the captain of the football team, and I was head cheerleader, so everyone thought we would be a perfect match. It seemed to me, though, that he was only interested in throwing touchdowns and getting ready to go away to Mississippi State after graduation. Anyway, I was plenty busy myself. We managed to go to the senior prom together, but it was only a week before graduation and we soon lost touch.

I figured it was for the best. In addition to everything else, I still had my three brothers to take care of, and there was a new baby in the house. I felt like I was starting over, just when I had my brothers half raised.

Mother certainly knew how shocked I was to

learn a baby would soon join the family. I thought I was almost finished raising the boys so I could finally concentrate on preparing for the spectacular career I planned on pursuing after college.

Mother and I were alone in the kitchen one day not long before the baby was due, peeling potatoes and getting supper ready for all the men in our family.

"Edith, your daddy and I would like for you to name your new brother or sister," she announced.

I looked at her—shocked—and then realized how thrilled that simple gesture had left me. I hugged her and told her I would do my best. It was a weighty responsibility. From my early attempts at writing, I knew how crucial it was to properly christen my characters, how much a name defined the person who carried it.

Well, I had always liked the name Kimberly. I had seen a movie with a character named Kimberly, and I combined that with Mother's name, Sue. We didn't get a chance to use the boy's name. So when my new little sister arrived, she was dubbed Kimberly Sue Blackburn. Mother seemed pleased that I had added Sue, and so did Daddy.

My brothers were good athletes. They played football, basketball, and baseball in high school. David was named Most Valuable Running Back in football his senior year and voted Class Clown in the yearbook. Terry had excelled in all three sports before his accident, and he was named Most Likely to Succeed. Phillip was a good baseball player, a hard-nosed infielder, and when he was at bat, he always seemed to find a way to get on base. He was also voted Most Handsome his senior year.

I was proud of them, proud as any momma. As big sister and nominal mom, it fell to my lot to drive them to and from practice and their other school events until they got their driver's licenses. I never missed their games, even when I wasn't required to lead cheers for them from the sidelines. Mother was often ill, and Daddy was usually at the Tennessee Valley Authority facility, running his general store in Burnout, or managing his fleet of trucks.

Grandma Alice would often go with me to their

games when there weren't cows to milk or a foal to birth or something else that required her presence. She loved baseball, especially when her grandsons were out there on the diamond. We found ourselves a spot in the bleachers and sat there talking when we weren't up on our feet, urging our boys on.

My grandmother was a remarkable woman: the mother of twelve kids and a true country philosopher. Her husband, Grandpa Walter, was a lumberman. Looking at her, you could imagine she had done her own share of saw milling. A big, stately lady, she was also a midwife and an unofficial but very efficient veterinarian. She delivered or helped with the birth of most of the people who lived in the little community of La Grange, near Russellville, and also with many of the horses, cows, and other farm animals. She had a special passion for animals, especially horses. There is no doubt that we inherited our own love for them from her.

Grandma Alice taught me how to cook and sew and do so much more. Dressed in her bonnet and apron, she took me to her barn and showed me how to milk the cows—even how to birth calves. Many of the recipes I later included in my cookbooks came from sessions in her wood-stove kitchen. Her classes in southern manners often became a fun dress-up party, with the costumes coming from her collection of exotic hats. She liked to put on "high teas," too, bringing a bit of London and England to rural northwest Alabama. We dined on her finest china and learned to hold our pinkies just right as we sipped tea from tiny, delicate cups. Imagine, such elegance from a lady who was just as comfortable foaling a pony in the back pasture as she was teaching a little girl the proper way to set a formal table.

Mainly, she taught me about faith and responsibility, about using whatever talents God had given me for His purposes. As we sat there on the bleachers at my brothers' baseball games, the cool breeze in our faces and the banter of the teams echoing around us, she talked to me about the things I would be required to do, whether I had yet chosen to accept the responsibility or not. They were not lectures. She spoke directly, confidently, simply, spelling out things I would have had to figure out on my own if not for her tutelage. She shared her common-sense philosophy of life just as certainly as she did her recipes and directions on how to stitch an intricate needlepoint pattern.

"You're special, Edith," she said. Then, after yelling a few choice words at the umpire, she went on. "You have real talent, darlin'. And I don't just mean your piano playin' and singing and how you write such pretty poems and stories. You know how to get next to people—in a good way—and then how to convince them to do the things they ought to do. And then you make 'em think they thought to do it in the first place. You can inspire, little girl. Inspire!"

Sometimes I shared my frustrations with her, of always having to be the momma for my brothers and sister. I told her how tired I got sometimes of having to cook and clean when I'd rather go to Florence to shop with my friends or hang out with boys at the drive-in at Sheffield or study my lines for the school play.

"I know it's hard, honey. But God is using you to shape those boys. Your little sister, too. They need you. So do your mother and daddy. Especially with all that's going on between them now. And remember, this life on earth is just a journey toward a wonderful destination in heaven. You may hit some rough spots in the road, but God will show you the way around them if you'll let Him. And when this ride is finally over, you can rest for eternity. There's plenty to enjoy along the way, don't forget." Then, suddenly she'd scream, "Hey, Ump! If that was a strike, my uncle's my dad blame aunt!"

I didn't necessarily believe her at the time. I didn't understand why all this responsibility had fallen to me. It was difficult, mothering a crew of rowdy boys and a new baby sister, especially since I was still only a kid myself. I felt as if I had hardly had a childhood at all.

Something else made it even more difficult. I knew I was losing my brothers, slowly but surely, to adulthood. Maybe losing them in other ways, too.

That was especially true of Phillip. My baby

brother seemed to be growing darker, moodier all the time. Sometimes, in a fit of anger if he didn't get to ride the horse he wanted or if he had to ride tandem with one of the rest of us, he would storm off and hide. Or when he was older, he'd blow up if one of the other boys took the car and he was left stranded, forced to walk to wherever he wanted to go.

"I don't belong here! I don't even think I'm part of this family!" he would scream.

Then he would skulk off to the woods until the mood lifted. Eventually he would return, acting as if nothing had happened.

Not long after Phillip turned thirteen, I saw just how slippery the tightrope was that he was walking.

It was a weekend night, well after midnight. Phillip was supposed to be out with his friends, playing basketball in the churchyard, and he was told to be home by ten. I heard him stumbling in, singing loudly and offkey. Phillip had a beautiful voice and often took the lead in our in-house concerts. I knew something was wrong, and I got up to see about him. It took only one whiff to confirm that he had been drinking. I steered him back out onto the porch and sat him down in the swing, hoping the damp, cool, night air would sober him up before he woke up Mother and Daddy.

I couldn't help it. I had to straighten him out.

"What do you mean, Phillip Blackburn? You know Daddy would kill you if he caught you drinking."

"Aw, leave me alone, big sis," he said, his words decidedly skewed. "I ain't had but only a can or two on account of we were thirsty."

He laid his head on my shoulder and was asleep—or passed out cold as a wedge—in a moment. I sat there, gently rocking the porch swing back and forth, letting him sleep. He was finally stable enough that I was able to help him inside and get him spread across his bed. I don't think our parents or my brothers ever knew about that night, and we didn't talk about it the next day.

The incident was over, but I would learn soon well enough that Phillip had a hurt that I could never fix with iodine and a bandage.

6

As we were growing up, I can honestly say that I loved all of my brothers and my sister equally. That being said, I also acknowledge that there was a special relationship between my brother David and me.

Maybe it was because we were the closest in age. Or because of his wit when things got rocky, or the way he could defuse any situation with sly humor and a broad wink. If Terry lost his temper or Phillip went silent and stony over nothing at all, or if I got a bit too bossy, David had a knack for reeling us back in with a joke, a silly facial expression, or the nonsensical but hilarious songs he seemed able to compose on the spot.

When we were young, he loved to climb aboard Spotted Cloud and gallop off, then come roaring back, now in character as the sheriff of Tombstone or as Sir Lancelot come to free Maid Marian from her evil kidnappers. Even when he went on to high school and his need for speed was filled by the fast cars he was drawn to, he still found time for our favorite pastime: riding the horses around our home place.

He was persistent. It seemed I was always busy trying to cram more and more into my day than would fit. He somehow managed to coax me away from my studies or housework or my weekend job at Jack's Drive-In or at Sherman's Department Store. All David had to do was twist his long curls up like pigtails, make a funny face, and use some weird voice to plead with me to go riding with him.

Once we were saddled up and off, he would let Spotted Cloud run as fast as she would go across the rolling green hills that stretched out in all directions from around our home place. I didn't even try to catch up with them, for I knew he would come racing back to meet me, already pretending to be a U.S. marshal or that we were exploring a planet in a distant galaxy.

Sometimes I wondered if he had come from another planet. He was different from the rest of us in so many ways. He never seemed to have a serious moment or get mad. We all loved to play, but he took his playing to a whole new creative level. I told him he had to decide whether he was going to be a comedian or a serious actor or a singer in a rock and roll band like our cousin. He just grinned and said, "Why not all those and more?"

At the far corner of the back pasture, a special oak tree seemed to reach all the way to the sky. That's where David and I usually ended up when our horses became winded or we had exhausted the plot line of our play-acting. The tree was close enough to the creek that the horses could drink while we stretched out in the shade of the broad branches and caught our own breath.

It was there in the shadow of that tree that we shared our special dreams, private ones that were even more personal than those we spun when we were with our younger brothers. These moments are my only memories I have of David even approaching becoming serious. He would get a faraway look in his big, brown eyes and a furrow in his brow, and he would talk unashamedly about what he wanted to do with his life.

Early on it was a different dream every time—spaceship captain, cowboy, police detective. Once we were in our teens, he stuck to the same scenario each time.

"I want a house, right up there on that hill," he would say, pointing to one of the highest points on our Daddy's land. "And a workshop out back. I'm going to build racecars and win races all over the country. I'll be as famous as Bobby Allison and Richard Petty put together. And Joann Ham will marry me, and we'll have more kids than Mrs. Magoo."

Joann was a tall, brown-haired girl who had caught David's attention back in junior high. She and

David skipped going steady altogether and became "engaged" when he was a sophomore and she a freshman in high school.

I always nodded and accepted his dream as reality. I didn't doubt for a moment that his hopes would come true. His were certainly no more far-fetched than mine. There was something about his sincerity, too, that left no doubt that David Blackburn would accomplish about anything he set his mind to. I wasn't so sure about me.

"I am going to clog dance on *Grand Ole Opry*," I told him, "and become a movie star. And I'm going to have my own television show, just like Dinah Shore."

David never laughed at me, even though my dreams sometimes seemed silly even to me, especially as we grew older and more realistic about the possibilities of seeing them come true. No, David just nodded solemnly as if to confirm that each and every fantasy would most certainly play out for me.

"What about kids?" he asked one day. I was about sixteen by then. "Edith, you never talk about having me any nieces and nephews."

I looked at him sideways, surprised he had even asked me. He knew I had too much to do to have a family holding me back.

"Oh, I won't have time for babies or a husband."

I remember him looking at me oddly, as if the being-a-star part was perfectly plausible, but not the last part. No way. Why would anybody not want a house full of sons and daughters?

"Edith, you know that's not so. You've been like a mother to us, and I bet you anything you can't just quit being one, no matter what." He stopped for a minute and watched a hawk soaring on the thermals off in the distance. I could hear crows cawing up a storm and a bluebird singing its heart out somewhere up in the tree branches. "Edith, you are going to do great things. I don't have any doubts about that. You have a way with people, too, and you'll use your gift to help them. You know how to give hope to folks who have lost all the hope they had. But you'll be a momma someday, too. You can count on that."

Then he was up, doing a hilarious, exaggerated impression of an Indian brave, sneaking up on Spotted Cloud and hopping aboard, urging her into a fast gallop. It was as if he was trying to get away as fast as he could from the approaching cavalry and all our solemn conversation. As usual, he was whooping and laughing as he went, loving the exhilaration that speed brought him. Loving life.

Lord, my baby brother loved life!

David was nineteen, in the spring of his freshman year of college at Florence State, now the University of North Alabama, where I was a senior getting ready for graduation. He and I shared a house together near campus. Terry had joined us there, too, even though he was only sixteen at the time. Our parents, along with Phillip and Kim, had moved to Indiana. Our Aunt Jackie and Uncle Joe lived up there. Uncle Joe owned a local car dealership and a successful pipefitting business, and he had convinced my dad to help him. It was a business opportunity for Daddy, and he was never able to turn down one of those, even if it meant uprooting his family from the home we had known for so long.

Joann was a senior in high school by then, and

David and she were already making serious marriage plans for the summer. He was always so active, studying and going to class at night, working his full-time job at Sunshine Mills during the day, and making the forty-five-minute drive back and forth to visit with his fiancée every chance he got. On that particular day, he had been going since before sun-up, just another in his busy life.

On the way home, he fell asleep behind the wheel and the car veered into a tree not a mile from Grandma and Grandpa Blackburn's place just past Red Bay Bottoms. There was no doubt he was driving too fast. That's just the way David drove. He was always in a hurry. He wasn't wearing a seat belt either, and his body was thrown through the windshield. He ended up on the opposite side of the roadway, past the culvert in a ditch, his body horribly broken and battered.

Our Aunt Linda, who was still a registered nurse at the hospital in Red Bay, was on her way to work that night and was the first person to come up on the wreck. However, David's car was so mangled, its lights shining off at a cockeyed angle in the dark, that she didn't realize it was her nephew's vehicle. Smoke and dust were everywhere and the radio was still blaring away, turned up loud to the rock-and-roll radio station.

It took Aunt Linda a minute to find him lying in the weeds next to the roadway. She still didn't recognize the broken, bleeding mass as her nephew, but she followed her training and went to work to try to help the injured young man. She did all she could do to stop the bleeding then flagged down the next car that came by. Only when they loaded him into the ambulance did she realize it was her nephew that she had been trying to bring back from the brink of death.

She later told me that he tried to speak when they got him to the hospital, but his tongue was cut so badly and he was so weak from loss of blood that he couldn't get the words out. Aunt Linda said he kept staring at her and only calmed down when she finally told him, "Edith is coming. We called Edith. She's on the way. Hold on."

It was true. Two friends of David's came to get me and told me that my brother had been in a horrible accident, but they wouldn't tell me just how badly he had been hurt. I just knew I had to get down there to see about him, to take care of him, as I knew I was supposed to do.

But I wouldn't be able to help him this time. David was pronounced dead a few hours after the crash. His wonderful shining spirit was snuffed out before it ever had the chance to illuminate the lives of other folks the way it had mine.

A piece of me died with David. I had lost more than a brother. I had lost my best friend. For a long while, I wasn't so sure my heart could stand the pain.

It took a lot of praying—from me and from those around me—to get through those dark, dark days.

Once again, my ride through life had hit an impossibly rough patch of highway, and I had no idea about the detour I was about to make.

7

AUNT LINDA MADE the decision to send David's body to the funeral home. The rest of the family gathered at Grandpa Blackburn's place. I had arrived at the hospital, asking for my brother, running from room to room to try to find him so I could take care of him.

A nurse I didn't know said, "Oh, David died. Every bone in his body was broken. It was terrible." She later lost her job for her callous words.

I couldn't believe what I was hearing, and I col-

95

lapsed to the floor, screaming uncontrollably. Two family friends, Jimmy Garrison and Alan Bostick, helped me to a little room and stayed with me until I could get hold of myself. Slowly, take-charge Edie emerged. and I realized I would have to be the one to deliver the news to Mother and Daddy and our brother and sister up in Indiana.

When Mom answered the phone, I only told her David had been in a wreck and asked if Daddy, Kim, and Phillip were there. She said they were. When I asked to speak to Daddy, she realized immediately that the news must be the worst. She begged me to tell her the truth, and when I finally did, I heard the telephone hit the floor.

Daddy was on the line then. Mother had fainted. Then I had to tell him the same awful news. I will never forget the awful wailing from him, Kim, and Phillip on the other end of that telephone line.

Then I knew I had to find Terry. He would need help, too. Strong as he was, this news would be enough to fell even an oak tree of a young man like him.

Friends drove me to Grandma Blackburn's house. There Terry and I held each other and cried until we couldn't cry anymore, drawing strength from each other along with the heartfelt condolences from all the others who found their way there that night.

Reality set in when Mother and Dad arrived the next day. They were a mess. I had to make all the decisions about the funeral, right down to what suit David was to be buried in.

So many things changed in that instant when David's car careened off that narrow stretch of road. My life took a sudden turn, and I made the decision not to finish college or to go to acting school in New York as I had planned for years. I would have to take a different ride if I was going to realize my dreams. Everyone around me needed me at home, and I suppose that deep inside I knew that I needed to be there, too.

I should be thankful that God kept me so wrapped up in college, work, and church. I was mostly able to lose myself in the swirl of it all. Still, there were times when I was angry with God for taking such a pure soul away from us. There were so many others who didn't live right, who didn't bring the joy David did to everyone he met. Why him? Why did God feel the need to snatch him away from us?

I tried to remember Grandma Alice's admonition that there were rough spots in life's journey and that we should just drive on, intent on reaching our destination. "God has a plan," she always said. "He has a reason. We don't always know what that reason is. That's where our faith comes in. And faith is like a muscle. The more you try it, the stronger it becomes."

As usual, she made perfect sense, but it still hurt so bad I would sometimes start sniffling in the middle of class or while waiting on a customer at the Village Shop in Muscle Shoals where I worked. I blamed it on allergies, a cold.

With help from my granny and my brothers and sister and my friends from school, I began to do better. My drama teacher, Gladys Shepherd, was won-

derful to me, too. I pretty much had myself convinced that I would live through losing my precious
brother.

"God doesn't give us a burden without also offer-
ing us the strength to carry it," Grandma Alice had
told me at David's funeral. And her words did offer
me considerable peace on that awful day and inspiration in the months afterward. I decided life was
worth living after all, that I would always have my
brother's memory with me, and that I should feel
blessed for the time we all had with him.

Knowing David, I'm sure he would have wanted
us to feel that way.

A few weeks after we buried David, I was in the
kitchen getting an early start on Easter dinner.
Mother had invited her brothers and sisters over, and
I was intent on cobbling together the best Southern
meal any of them had ever seen. I wanted to get
most of the feast well underway before all the other
cooks in the family came in and tried to tell me how
to do it their way. I had pots and pans rattling, flour
all over the counter, a massive ham soaking up my

special pineapple glaze on the stove-top, and a couple of dozen yeast rolls swelling up beautifully in a pan on the windowsill.

The sun seemed to be shining especially bright that Easter Sunday. The birds' songs were extra sweet, too. Easter meant rebirth, a new day, a new hope. My heart still ached for David, but I was definitely feeling new hope as I prepared the meal that morning for all the company that would be coming.

I didn't know Mother was standing behind me until she spoke.

"Why weren't you there with him?" she asked me, her words cracking dryly.

"Ma'am?"

"Why weren't you taking care of David?"

"What do you mean, Mother?" I didn't understand what she was asking me. How could I have been out there on that highway with him? What could I have done to prevent that horrible accident?

"You know you were supposed to be taking care of him." Her voice was husky and hoarse. "That's what you were supposed to be doing. If you had been doing what you were supposed to be doing, he would be all right now. He'd be here for Easter dinner and not over yonder in that cold grave."

Then she burst into tears and ran back to her room, her wailing sobs audible until she slammed the door shut behind her.

I was numb and my knees were weak. I didn't know how to take the hurtful words she had unleashed on me. Suddenly unable to stand, I eased down into one of the kitchen chairs, kneaded my temples, and tried to keep calm. I struggled to understand why my mother had lashed out at me that way.

How could she say those hurtful things? How could my own mother blame me for what had happened? Irrational as her words were, they still hurt like wasp stings. My head was spinning, and I was afraid I was going to be sick.

I looked around, searching for someone who might help me answer those questions. There was no one there, of course.

But then, right there in our kitchen, surrounded by the smells of cooking food, the warmth from the stove, the shafts of sunlight streaming through the window, and the soft music I had been listening to on the radio, a strange calm swept over me. I couldn't imagine where it came from, but I welcomed it.

On some level, I knew that I should have screamed back at my mother, letting her know it was not my fault David had been killed. I should have followed her to her room, I thought, and defended myself, striking back at her to get even for the awful pain and guilt she had inflicted on me. After all, she was his mother. Why had she not . . . ?

But that was not the message I was receiving.

It was as if God put a hand on my shoulder, taking away the sting and softening the hard edge of my anger. Or as if my brother David were there in the kitchen with me, using that wonderful manner of his to put a balm on my raw feelings.

Then I understood, with wisdom far beyond my years and experience. It seemed as if God was taking the time from His busy schedule to put the puzzle pieces together for me.

Bless her heart, my mother was feeling the same

frustration as all of us at the loss of our beloved David. The rest of us—Daddy, Terry, Phillip, Kim, me—we all had within us the strength to bear the pain.

My mother did not.

Her only outlet was to confront me, to blame and accuse me, to say those awful words to me. That was her way of purging the anguish she couldn't cast off any other way. It was the only way she could heal.

Somehow she knew that I could take it, that I would find the armor to shield myself from her words, and she was right. There, among the fixings for our Easter dinner, I had.

When the time was right, I would talk with her and let her know I loved her, that I didn't hold against her the way she dealt with her horrible pain any more than I could hold her accountable for her blinding headaches or stifling depression.

If blaming me, as misplaced as it was, helped her cope with her loss, then I was going to allow God to make me strong enough to bear it.

Then I cried for a good half hour, allowing the

hurt to pour out of me with every teardrop.

Soon the yeast rolls were ready to go into the oven and the potatoes had boiled enough to mash, and I went back to cooking, just the way my Grandma Alice had taught me to.

8

DAVID WAS RIGHT, of course, when he told me I would one day marry.

Just when I least expected it—and had the least amount of time for such foolishness—I fell in love with a gentle older man named Lincoln. We talked about children at some point, but we were both too busy to seriously consider such a commitment. I was just out of college, working at the University of Alabama in Birmingham, employed by Dr. Buris Boshell, the founder of a widely respected diabetes hospital. Lincoln was ten years my senior and already a successful businessman.

With most of my family except for Kim now grown and with my brand new husband by my side, I began pursuing my girlhood ambitions with a vengeance. It seemed sometimes that I was trying to prove something to my brothers, Terry and Phillip. I wanted to show them that I could make it happen almost exactly the way I had described it to them as we lay on our bellies in the green grass atop the old Indian mounds. They had never scoffed or doubted, but I felt the need to show them anyway.

Not long out of college, I used some contacts I made through Dr. Boshell to form my own advertising agency. I signed up as clients some of the same companies I did voice work and copywriting for while I was still in school. I loved the creative aspect of the business. It was just like making up some of those elaborate stories when my brothers and I had played in the pasture. The artistic side of the agency was beginning to prosper, and my husband did what he could to help me handle the business end. That wasn't my favorite part, and it was certainly more of a challenge. I enjoyed writing and recording the jingles, coming up with clever ways to call attention to the products and services that my clients offered, and working with television stations to produce the commercials. But when it came to drawing up contracts, buying the ads, paying the invoices, making sure the billing was correct, and trying to get paid by my clients, I tried to put off as much of it as I could.

Despite the continual whirlwind, so many wonderful, creative people kept popping up like bright lights along the roadway. I was amazed at how they were so willing to share their knowledge and advice with a country girl from Burnout, Alabama.

Then another twist appeared in the path on which I was riding. I had been having pain in my right side, and it was discovered that I had kidney stones. No problem. If I could stand the pain and take my pills, it would be fine and I could continue working. But then it became much more complicated and downright terrifying.

At only twenty-six years old, I discovered I had a

rare kidney disease and cancer. My doctor, Karl Hofammann, performed major surgery, removing a kidney and half of the other one.

After the surgery, Dr. Hofammann was concerned that I was not regaining strength as quickly as I should have been. That is when he discovered that I was pregnant. Because of all the drugs I had been getting, and due to my weakened condition, the decision was made to take the child.

That was not all. I would likely never be able to get pregnant again.

I cried, and I prayed. I leaned on my husband and on my brothers. And I vowed to carry on as best I could, even along this rocky stretch of road.

Only four years later, we were blessed with Lincoln Addison Hand, a nine-pound, seven-ounce baby boy. Linc was my miracle baby, a gift from the Lord.

I had the good fortune to meet some people who did casting in New York for television, and they offered me some work with the promise of more to come. I met Anne Sward, a regular on *As the World Turns*, the long-running daytime drama. She put in a good word for me, and before I knew it, I had a recurring role on the show and offers to do more.

I was active in an organization called American Women in Radio and Television, and there I met Dr. Judy Kuriansky, a brilliant clinical psychologist and sex therapist at Columbia University in New York. She put her considerable performing talent to work helping people through her radio and TV programs. She graciously invited me to sit in on her shows and taught me about communicating through the microphone and camera.

We later created our own TV show called *Total Wellness for Women*. I was on my way, and the rough ride I had been on seemed to have finally smoothed out.

Linc went to a Christian school in Birmingham that was only a few steps away from my office. It was easy to pick him up after class, and we fixed up a special area in the office for him for when school was out. He had his own space and even starred in some of the commercials for one of my larger clients, Sunshine Foods.

Several people from the area where I grew up had made it big in Nashville, and I was not at all bashful about renewing those old friendships. Everywhere I went up and down Music Row, it seemed that someone from back home was already there welcoming me. Buddy Killen, one of the most prolific music producers and writers in the business, became a best friend. So did Judy Spencer Nelon, owner of one of the top gospel music publishing companies in Music City.

Soon, and to my amazement, I was rubbing elbows with important, famous people in New York, Los Angeles, and Nashville. It was exhilarating stuff for a little blonde-haired girl from the sticks, but I vowed not to miss out on the opportunities such relationships offered me.

My husband, baby Linc, and I decided to move to Nashville. I was poised to take on the entertainment business and let them all know to watch out— Edie had arrived. God had blessed me. I wasn't going to disappoint Him, even if I was too busy most of the time to thank Him. I rarely made church, but I figured God would understand sixty-hour work weeks.

I suppose I was so wrapped up in proving to everyone that I could make it in some of the toughest businesses there are that I didn't notice some things. My marriage and my own health were both suffering. My husband and I rarely saw each other, let alone talked, but things were going so well with my career. I hardly noticed the growing distance between us. Even worse, because of the limited time I had for him, Linc spent more time with his dad than with me. That was not the way I wanted it to be. Nor was it the way it was supposed to be.

Just when I thought things couldn't get any better, that I was invincible, I developed a nagging backache. On some mornings it was hard to climb out of bed to make it to meetings or rehearsals or video shoots. The pain simply wouldn't go away with aspirin or analgesic cream or when I tried to ignore it.

My husband finally convinced me to visit a doctor. I had always avoided physicians if at all possible.

They usually preached slowing down, taking it easy, giving up some of the many jobs I held until whatever my ailment was went away. Instead, what I wanted from them was a shot in the hip and a twice-a-day pill I could take to get better without having to slack off one bit.

I had too many worlds to conquer. I didn't have time to pass a kidney stone or recuperate from some pesky infection.

I knew it wasn't good news when I saw the expression on the doctor's face.

"You have cancer again, Edie. This time it is uterine," he said, not sugarcoating it at all. "We're going to have surgery, and we'll try to maintain your ability to have children. But we can't mess with this stuff. It's serious. If we don't do this now, the cancer will metastasize and spread into other parts of the body. I have to be honest with you. It may have already."

"Am I going to die?"

"Sure. Everybody does. But we'll do all we can to make sure it's a long way down the road for you, Edie."

My mother-in-law, Margie, and my husband, Lincoln, were with me the whole trip, as usual. They stuck beside me and helped with the whole experience. Margie took care of Linc and allowed me to put more time and effort into my recovery and still be able to work some in my businesses. She was a very special grandma.

God was with me, too. So were Phillip, Terry, and Kim.

Between them all, they kept me on an even keel through the pain and scars and therapy. I never doubted I would beat the cancer. Phillip, Terry, and Kim were especially adamant about keeping me cheered up, not allowing any doubts to creep in. As soon as the soreness allowed, they took me back to Burnout for a few days of recuperation. They had me up on a horse the first day, walking her gingerly down to the "blue hole" so we could wade in the clear, cool water looking for minnows like a quartet of kids.

Though my whole body ached and the chemo made me retch for a couple of days after each round, those rides made me feel better, reassuring me I would beat the cancer. So did my nightly conversations with God as I lay in my childhood bed.

With their help and the realization that my little boy needed me, I fought as hard as I could to get better. I will never forget the day when my husband and little Linc brought me a dozen yellow roses. My son looked up at me with those beautiful, clear eyes and asked, "Momma, are you going to die?"

I was not lying to my son when I told him—in no uncertain terms—"No!"

I knew that I wasn't. The doctors and treatments were going to help me get better. My family, with their prayers and their good wishes, were doing the same.

But there was one more punch waiting, and it came on one of my first visits back to my oncologist. He was honest and straightforward with me on that score, too.

"Edie, after all this, you will never be able to have any more children."

I accepted the finality of something I already had

suspected. I merely nodded and thanked him for keeping me alive. I assured him I wouldn't need the box of tissues he offered me. After all, I had told my dear brother David, right out there beneath our special tree where no untruths were allowed, that I had no intention of raising a second set of young'uns after I got him and his siblings grown. Still, as soon as I was out of the doctor's office and back on the street toward home, I started crying and couldn't quit. Somehow I managed to pull into the parking lot next to Nashville's replica of the Greek Parthenon.

A young mother and her two children were near the duck pond, feeding the birds bits of stale bread. Another mother pushed her little girl on one of the swings in the park.

Why, God? I cried. Surely you know my heart, know that I secretly wanted more children. But then I realized—and maybe it was God's voice speaking to me—that it wasn't meant to be.

Just as had happened in the past, I felt a strong hand on my shoulder. The agonizing disappointment seemed to melt away.

I would accept this, however it played out. It was just another bump in the road, something I would have to find the strength to steer past. So once again I decided I'd just drive on and see what was waiting around the next bend in the road. And I'd let God have His way.

As soon as I was able, I put my lipstick on, colored my cheeks, and threw myself back into my work. The Lord continued to bless me. I landed some roles on several soap operas and used that exposure to make my ad agency more viable. Still, when I did a commercial shoot for a client that used a couple of little girls as actors, I felt a tug at my heart. They were blonde and handsome and full of mischief like my brothers. I was "Aunt Edie" to a couple of friends' kids, too. A couple of them were boys, and they reminded me so much of my brothers and of some of the antics they used to pull. I kept telling myself that it was far better to play with them and send them home, to buy them birthday presents and not have to clean up the messes, than it would have been to juggle all that responsibility once again.

Not with all I had to accomplish. I had been a momma as long as I could remember.

Meanwhile Linc was growing into a very artistic child. He loved baseball, and his dad was his coach. He also had a liking for exotic animals. We had an iguana as the baseball team mascot and, of course, the critter wore a rhinestone collar. That blessed iguana ate better than I did! I know because I had to cook the ugly thing's dinner in the microwave.

Terry, Phillip, and Kim had been among the first to come visit when we got my son home from the hospital. I couldn't believe how goofy my brothers acted over their new nephew. Terry, who had gone into the contracting business, made him a beautiful cradle out of cedar and hung a miniature football above it, "So he can get an early start," he said. "He looks like a quarterback to me." He had artfully carved perfect horseshoes into the head and foot of the bed. "Same size as Trigger's. I used one of her old shoes for the pattern," Terry said with a wink when he saw me admiring his handiwork. Trigger had been "my" horse.

Phillip made funny faces at the baby and promised to teach him how to ride as soon as he was big enough to sit up on a horse. His gift was a little guitar with Linc's initials inscribed on the neck. In baby talk, Phillip told my son that he would have him wailing away on the instrument before he started talking.

Phillip was now working with Terry in his contracting business. I thought he looked as happy and animated that day as I had ever seen him. But I also noticed his cheeks were flushed, his eyes red. I tried not to think it, but I suspected he had been drinking before he got to our house.

I could only hope Linc would have as memorable a childhood as we all did, that he had inherited the practical abilities and talents of his uncles, as well as their fertile imagination.

My rocky ride through life had taken me up a couple of steep climbs and, with the help of God and those I loved the most, it seemed that I had now made it over the top. Though my husband and I were still having problems, we were trying to

work through them, as much for our son as for ourselves.

I couldn't believe how fulfilled I now felt. My
career was very important to me. It always would be,
but not nearly so much as doting on my son, seeing
to his every need, watching him grow.

Maybe we were finally in for a long, downhill
glide. As if to confirm it, there would soon be one
more bit of good news to come my way.

It would be a bona fide miracle, and it would be
exactly what was required for me to make it past the
next unexpected barrier on my life's journey.

9

GOD WAS BLESSING me mightily. Just as Grandma Alice had said, all the things I had been through had strengthened me, and so would my growing relationship with Christ.

In addition to my recurring roles on a couple of top-rated daytime dramas, my agency was doing well, and I had signed an agreement to host and produce a nationally syndicated television show. I was busy with my career, being a mom, and trying to do it all. Time flew past in a blur.

In the midst of it all, I received a middle-of-the-night telephone call that brought some wonderful news from back home about Phillip—how far he had fallen and the wonderful rebirth he had undergone.

Phillip told me the entire story a few weeks later. He was a bit shy but still beamed as he sat in my living room in Nashville. He cried happy tears as he held my son on his knee and played "horsey" with him while he talked about what had happened to him.

He confessed that his drinking had gotten even worse than I had suspected. Terry had been threatening to take him somewhere to get him help, but he knew that Phillip would ultimately have to want that help if it was to do him any good. He had begun to miss work, leaving Terry's thriving construction business in the lurch, and a blow-up was almost certainly due. Terry took the quality and timeliness of his work seriously, and it was clear he was getting near the end of his rope with Phillip, even if he was our baby brother.

Phillip had married young, too. He had a beautiful daughter named Tyann Michelle. We called her "Muffin" because she was a carrot top—a carrot top muffin! Phillip's wife left him when Muffin was only six months old, and our sister, Kim, came home to help him take care of her. I did not know it then, but God was lining up people for what was about to happen.

Meanwhile, Phillip had gone back to his wild ways. He ran with a rough crowd of friends, jumping from bar to bar and party to party. Whatever he was looking for, he clearly was not finding whatever was missing in his life. In spite of all that, my brother was still a warm and sensitive guy trying to be a good father and attempting to give Muffin a good life while struggling to find himself.

Then one rainy, stormy Sunday night, Phillip lost control of his car and ran off the road, striking the edge of a culvert. Even though he had been thrown hard into the steering wheel, he was okay. Just sore. I suppose it's true what they say about God watching over drunks and children. It turned out He had other plans for Phillip that evening.

Even to someone as inebriated as Phillip, it was obvious the car wasn't going anywhere. The tire was blown and the axle bent, and there was no way to drive it out of that muddy ditch.

He sat down in the middle of the road and laughed crazily, waiting for someone to come along and help him, but nobody did. Finally, cold and wet and slowly sobering up, he began to walk, looking for a farmhouse with a telephone he could use to call a friend or uncle to come get him. Maybe it wouldn't be too late to make it to the other party after all. He would worry about his car later. Right now, there was drinking and singing to be done.

Phillip walked for several miles before he saw a dim light in the distance, shimmering in the misty raindrops, but it was no farmhouse. Instead, it was a small country church with a scattering of a dozen or so cars out front. Phillip could hear piano music and the singing of a choir.

He had forgotten it was Sunday night. Church was still going on.

Though he wasn't in the mood for listening to

any preaching, he was now sober enough to realize that it would be warmer and dryer inside. Maybe after the services were over, someone would give him a lift home.

As Phillip neared the parking lot in front of the building, he realized that the little white church looked familiar. So did the simple images of a welcoming Jesus, arms extended to all who would come, etched on the two stained-glass windows at its front.

Of course! He had been here before.

This was the church at Bessadea, a little community about ten miles from Russellville. Grandma Alice had taken Phillip and the rest of us there several times when we were kids. Once we watched a baptism service held in the little creek that flowed behind the church.

David had joked about the water moccasins being the main ones who got baptized in that snaky creek, that he wouldn't be surprised to see an alligator join in the service and sing along with the choir. Grandma Alice had to pinch him hard on the fleshy part of his arm to get him to hush his silliness so we would quit our giggling.

Now that he knew where he was, Phillip felt better about his chances of getting some help. The church probably wouldn't have a telephone, but somebody would surely know Daddy or Grandma Alice and be willing to take him to one. He pushed open the door and stepped inside, hoping not to call attention to himself. He was wet and filthy, and he knew he reeked of cigarette smoke and whiskey. But it was warm inside. He found a spot on the last row of pews and sat down, hoping no one—and especially the preacher—had seen him come in.

But then, without even realizing he was doing it, he began to join in with the familiar hymns the congregation was singing. He was surprised he still remembered the words to the songs. They came back to him even though it had been years since he had been inside a church. And when the preacher began his message, Phillip even remembered some of the biblical passages he quoted. He was amazed that, still half-drunk or not, they seemed to make uncommon good sense to him.

"Edith, it was like he was talking to me, not to any of those other folks there," he said as he sat in my den and rocked his little girl. "He prepared that sermon especially for me. Every word was aimed straight at my heart. And he was telling the truth."

As my brother recounted his story, I couldn't help but notice the glow in his eyes and the color in his cheeks. I knew this time it was not the result of alcohol.

In some ways, Phillip had always been the most loving of my brothers. He was a young man with a good soul—a wonderful heart—and a seemingly infinite capacity for caring, even if those traits were sometimes hidden by his moodiness and his proclivity for drowning his feelings with strong drink.

Phillip told about how, as he stood there singing, a warm feeling came over him even as he still shivered inside his wet, muddy clothes. Before he knew it, the congregation was on its feet, singing the invitational, the call to the altar for those who would be

saved. It was another song he knew well, "Softly and Tenderly."

As the words rang out around him, as he sang the harmony part of the song as loud and on key as he ever had, he suddenly felt as if his heart was going to burst. He seemed to have lost control of his legs. They moved on their own and carried him the length of the pew and right out into the aisle.

Tears streamed down his cheeks as he stepped from the anonymity of the back row of the church and slowly walked toward the front where the minister waited for him and welcomed him with a big smile and open arms.

Right there, in that little country church, Phillip Blackburn came to the Lord and turned his life around. The church members provided him hot coffee, food, and dry clothes, and the preacher gave him a lift to Grandma Alice's house to spend the night.

It was from there that they both got on the telephone and called me. It was near midnight, but they couldn't wait until morning to tell me the good news.

I was skeptical when I heard what had happened. I loved my brother with all my heart, but Terry had filled me in on many of the details of how far he had fallen. Could one experience in a country church stem the downward spiral that Phillip was on? I certainly had my doubts.

It could. And it did.

My brother was a changed man.

That day in my living room, he cried and apologized for all he had done to worry me and the rest of the family.

"Edith, you have been the most wonderful sister any man could want," he told me. "I knew all along the things you sacrificed so you could help raise us. And I want you to know how sorry I am that I made it more difficult for you and for Terry with all my drinking and carrying on."

"That's over, honey," was all I could think to say. "You've got a straight road ahead. Be a good daddy to Muffin. You do that, and it will make up for everything that has happened and all the time you've missed with her."

As I watched him back out of my driveway and head back toward home, I felt relief, of course. More important, though, was the realization that for the first time since Phillip was born, I no longer felt the responsibility of raising him and keeping him safe.

He had finally become a man and a father. He was in God's hands now.

10

THREE MONTHS TO the day after Phillip came to see
me, a family from his new church was visiting with
him at my mom and dad's home in Muscle Shoals.
Before they sat down to dinner, Muffin mentioned
that she wished she had a fast food hamburger
instead of the meatloaf that was being served for the
meal.

As usual, Phillip was ready to give her about
anything she wanted. Maybe that was his way of
making up for his neglect over the years.

Another friend of Phillip's was there as well, and he offered to drive Phillip to the nearest fast food place. They could visit some more along the way.

As they passed through a busy intersection two blocks from home, an eighteen-wheeler ran a stoplight and slammed into the passenger side of the car, where Phillip rode.

My precious baby brother was killed instantly.

11

THERE WERE DAYS when I was certain my life was becoming a bigger soap opera than those I was in on television. Like many who lose someone they love too early, once again I threw myself into my work after we buried Phillip, mostly to forget what had happened. However, I was still so driven to succeed, especially after being so brutally reminded once more that life's journey is often shorter than we expect.

It slowly dawned on me that no matter how I

was keeping score on my accomplishments, the tally was coming at a high price. I was once more neglecting the people I loved, those still on this earth who depended on me: my husband, son, brother and sister, and parents. Even my employees at my advertising agency.

Unfortunately, I realized this too late to save my marriage. My husband and I divorced, and suddenly I was a single mother. My ex-husband and his parents remained a big part of Linc's life and took care of him often so I could maintain the lifestyle to which I had been drawn. Somehow, and oddly enough, it seemed like a very familiar role to me. Then I realized why.

It was almost like being back home again, raising my brothers.

I felt another strong calling, too. It was too loud and persistent to ignore.

Grandma Alice had instilled in me the desire to use whatever abilities I had to help others, to give hope to people who had lost all hope. So had David that day beneath the embracing branches of our special tree. Losing Phillip so tragically, so unexpectedly, gave me the final push I needed to get it done.

I decided to use my contacts in the media and my God-given public speaking ability to do something positive for those less fortunate. Grandma Alice kept telling me I could coax a dog into climbing a tree if I put my mind to it, and I decided to see if she knew what she was talking about.

I didn't know exactly what a foundation was or how a person went about starting one, but I did it anyway. I set it up to raise money to assist charitable organizations in meeting the needs of their communities, to help those who were least able to help themselves. I took special interest in charities that help kids with cancer and juvenile diabetes.

Almost immediately, and usually without being asked, many of my friends in the entertainment industry pitched in to help. They did concerts, donated profits from songs they had written, mentioned the foundation in their media interviews, and did all they could to get it off on a strong footing.

I had been fortunate with my own bouts with

cancer, and I knew a lot about what these kids and their families were going through. I also knew I wanted to help in any way I could to make the journey easier for them.

God had shown me a way to do that. He made me stronger after the deaths of my two brothers. He had shown me the way through the travails of my cancer, had allowed me to live out many of my childhood dreams, and had given me a wonderful son.

All I did was take what He gave me and run with it. I had no intentions of looking back.

12

But God wasn't finished testing me yet.

I found myself, again, in front of grim-faced doctors who told me that I had cancer again. The first time it was in the kidneys. The second was uterine. Now a small lump in my left breast was malignant but apparently had not yet metastasized. Prayer, friends, and family had seen me through in the past. My brother, Terry, was with me all the way, as were my sister and parents. I knew that Kim and her two daughters, Kristi and Kayla, along with my own Linc, would give me courage to face another dark turn in the road. The only thing I knew to do was to keep riding. I truly believe my survival is due to my faith, my family, and my belief that my work on this earth was not yet finished.

To be sure, there was more pain and sickness and scars, both visible and emotional, but those brushes with my own mortality only spurred me to run harder, to cram as much ride into the day as I could manage. The foundation became even more important for me. I desperately wanted to ease the pain of every suffering person I met, whether or not it was a practical goal for me.

Inevitably, though, that commitment was gradually overshadowed by my continuing drive to succeed in the business world. Even when chemo and surgery left me weak, depressed, and feeling sorry for myself, I still made trips to New York and Los Angeles, pitched accounts, and hosted radio and TV shows. I was also busy on a series of cookbooks, and the publisher was not interested in any excuses for

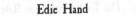

why the galleys were late or for why we didn't get the recipes tested on time.

If God wanted me to do wonderful things, who was I to let self-pity or sickness slow me down? I simply gave the horse a spur in the flank and rode on as hard as I could. My faith had been tested, but I had acquired the knack of finding inspiration when I most needed it.

But there was one more test coming, and it would be the biggest hurdle yet.

13

I WAS IN my kitchen at home when the telephone call came. Terry was very sick.

I had no idea he had gone downhill so quickly. We had seen each other over the holidays. We'd had a great Christmas together and, along with Kim, had taken our traditional ride together to fetch the tree.

It had been an especially beautiful tree that year. We did our usual Christmas concert as we gathered around it and exchanged gifts. We sorely missed David and Phillip, but Mother and her new husband, Tom, along with Daddy and Kim and her family, were there. Without even realizing it, Linc was taking the part of David, entertaining everyone with his practical jokes and offbeat sense of humor.

Terry looked tired, but he said work had been keeping him awfully busy lately, that the stress of keeping up with the demand was sometimes causing him to have blinding migraine headaches. He had built his own house on nights and weekends, and that had prevented him from getting enough rest. It kept him away from his horses, too, and that bothered him. Nowadays, he said, the crush of business was continuous. It seemed like everybody suddenly wanted to move to our little rural community, and when they did, they wanted Terry Blackburn to build their homes. It was difficult to say no in a sellers' market.

On the phone that day, Terry told me the news himself in his usual direct manner. It was a tumor, growing out of control in his brain like some crazy dandelion weed. The pressure of the thing was robbing him quickly of all his motor functions. He was going down to Birmingham to look at his options for treatment. Only then would the doctors know what high hurdles he would be facing for the rest of his life, if he even survived the lengthy and involved operation. There was always the threat that the surgery could leave him in a coma, or that he could lose the ability to talk. He wanted me to be at his side.

"Sis, dying may not be the worst thing when you got a deal like this," he told me, his voice dull and resolved.

"Don't say that, dear," I shot back. "We'll beat this thing. You've been here every time I've needed you, and you know I'll be there with you."

"I know. And I hope you know how much I appreciate everything you've done. Everything you are about to do." I could picture his serious, brown eyes, now clouded with pain and fear. I wanted to be there with him that very minute. "We'll just take it one step at a time. We don't know how this trip is going to play out."

"We never do, Terry. But we'll do our best."

The words were so inadequate.

Kim, Mother, Dad, and I drove Terry down to Birmingham the day before his surgery. The morning was dark, cold, and dreary, with rain clouds hanging low above us. Even if it had been bright, sunny, and warm outside, I'm sure I would remember it as a miserable day. We hardly talked on the ride down, but as the downtown skyscrapers of Birmingham came in sight, Terry turned to me and handed me something he had been holding in his hand since we had gotten into the car back home. I couldn't tell what it was, but I instinctively took it.

"Please keep this for me," he said and quickly turned back to watch the trees rushing past, other cars whizzing by as if all was right with the world.

I looked at the object he had given me. It was a big beautiful horseshoe ring.

"What do I do with this?" I asked.

"I don't know, Edith," he said, and there was an odd look in his eyes. Not the familiar look of pain, but something much different. "Just keep it for me until this is over with. I want to give it to someone with a clean and pure heart. I'll let you know."

Someone with a clean, pure heart? That came from Psalms 51:10, Terry's favorite passage. "Create in me a pure heart, O God; and renew a steadfast spirit within me."

"Okay."

And God help me, the first thought I had was, What if he doesn't make it through surgery? What would I do with this ring? Who would I give it to for him if the surgery did not go well?

I know I'm not the first person to experience the feelings I had the next day when they wheeled my brother's gurney out of his room at University Hospital and down the long hallway toward the operating suite. But I'll never forget the look of fear on his pale face, the pain in his eyes, or the grim set of his lips.

Terry was scared. I had not seen fear on his face since he was five or six and a close bolt of lightning set off a horrendous peal of thunder. Or when he was twelve years old and learning to crawl and walk again after his accident.

He cried and grabbed me, shaking.

"Don't be afraid, Terry. It's just God's angels

rolling watermelons around heaven," I told him. I believed it, too, because Grandma Alice told me the same thing when a clap of thunder frightened me one day at her house. "You remember Grandma Alice telling us that. She is in heaven now, you know, with David and Phillip. Don't worry 'cause I'm heading to the chapel now. All the angels will be taking this ride with you while you are in surgery."

A look of peace came over his face, and he smiled ever so slightly.

That morning at the hospital, I didn't want to allow the double doors to swallow up my brother. I knew it was possibile that I was seeing Terry alive for the last time. He would certainly not be the same old Terry, even if he did come back out alive.

I understood, though, that I had to let him go to the operating room. It was his only chance for a longer life on this earth. I couldn't protect him from this thing no matter how desperately I wanted to.

I bent to kiss him one more time before I moved aside and let my sister and parents and his sons Terry and Davey say their last good wishes, too.

"Little brother, Terry," I said. "I wish you more courage than you have ever known. We're praying for you and God will be with you on this ride. You'll see."

"Thanks, Sis."

"And I'll make you a promise," I said. I don't know where the idea came from. I had certainly not been thinking about it or planning it. But I blurted it out before I had time to consider whether I could keep the promise or not. "You and I will take a Christmas ride again soon, just like when we were kids, so you come on back to us."

He smiled then, a crooked grin, and he flashed me that familiar wink. It appeared to me that all the dread left his eyes at that moment. Maybe it was only the medicine taking hold at last and relaxing him, but he pursed his lips and gave the slightest of nods.

"I'll hold you to that," he whispered. "I'll hold you to it."

And with that, he was gone.

14

I WENT STRAIGHT from the hallway to the little chapel on the hospital's second floor. My lips moved in prayer all the way, then in the chapel I got down on my knees and made a few more very powerful promises. This time they were to God, and I pledged I would keep them if He would only let my brother come through this. One of those vows was a reaffirmation that I would take Terry riding on his beloved quarter horse, Blacky, as soon as he was able to sit in the saddle.

And if for some reason God didn't see fit to let him survive the surgery, I begged Him to allow Terry to gently cross over to a place where the pastures were always green, the breeze perfumed by honeysuckle, the swimming hole cold, and the summer shade from the tall oaks broad and welcoming.

I was still on my knees in the chapel two hours later praying when Kim came to get me. Terry was in trouble. The nurse had asked all to come to the surgical waiting room.

The frustration in the doctor's words was clear as he talked to my mother and daddy, my sister, and me.

"Folks, I've failed Terry. The tumor is too deep. It is in the middle of his brain and, in trying to get it, I have already cost him his hearing and eyesight on one side." He paused for a breath. "We're not finished but I have to stop for now or we'll lose him for sure. If I don't go back in within the next twenty-four hours to relieve the pressure, he will certainly die."

We were too spent to do more than slump back

in our chairs and cry softly. We had known that this outcome was a definite possibility, but none of us had allowed ourselves to think of anything but the best outcome.

"Doctor Fisher, what are his chances of a normal life if he does survive?" I finally found the strength to ask.

"Edie, I don't know. I really don't know."

Tears streamed down Dr. Fisher's face now. I had never seen a surgeon cry, and it had a powerful effect on me. Apparently this distinguished physician, a professional who was supposed to remain aloof from his patients, had gotten to know my brother the way I knew him.

"May we see him?" I asked.

He broke several hospital rules when he said that we could. He warned us that Terry would be groggy from the anesthesia and probably in much pain, but they couldn't give him anything else because of the impending second surgery.

Even though we were forewarned, I couldn't believe what we saw when we walked into that

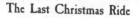
room. My brother's face was twisted in agony, his strong arms bound and tied down to keep him from clawing at the incision on top of his head. His hair had been shaved completely and he looked so small and vulnerable without the beautiful mane that he always kept so neatly combed. There were tubes and probes and IV lines strung everywhere.

"Edith, help me!" Terry groaned when he spotted me.

A sharp shaft of pain shot through me. There was nothing I could do. Nothing.

I touched Terry's face and wiped away his tears as I fell on my knees to beg God to intervene, one way or the other. My heart was breaking. Here I was again, the big sister who had always been able to help ease my siblings' aches and pains, and again I was helpless.

Terry told me, "I think I know now what Jesus Christ felt like when he was nailed to the cross. Please Edith, help me. Help me."

Now all I could do was pray.

My sister and I stayed with Terry the first night,

taking turns wiping his brow with a cold washcloth and swabbing his cracked, dry lips. When he was taken away early the next morning for the second operation, I went straight back to the chapel. God had kept his end of the bargain so far. Terry was still with us. I had to see what I could do to try to keep him around for that Christmas ride I had promised.

The news was still not good after the doctors completed the second surgery. They had removed as much of the tumor as they could get, but there had been unavoidable damage to his brain. Terry would be confined to a wheelchair. He had lost most of the ability to move by himself, and he had blurred vision and could hear from only one ear. There was no way to tell yet if the remaining parts of the tumor might regenerate or how aggressively it would spread if it did.

I was sitting in the chair in Terry's room, fighting sleep, trying to read my Bible, when he opened his eyes.

"I'm still here?" he wondered, his voice raspy and disbelieving.

"Yes, you are, dear! Yes, you are."

Somehow he managed a small, uneven smile.

"Too tough to die, I guess," he whispered, and then dozed off again.

Later that day, he woke me up from a fitful nap. He asked me to come closer to him.

"What did you do with the horseshoe ring I gave you?" he asked.

"It's right here, around my neck, on the chain with my cross necklace." I showed it to him. I had put it there to make sure I didn't lose it. I had held it in my hand for hours during his two surgeries while I prayed for him. If I couldn't hold his hand, I'd do the next best thing. "Have you decided what you want me to do with it, Terry?"

"Yes, I have." There were tears in his eyes. I gently wiped them away with a tissue. "My dear sister, I want you to keep my golden horseshoe." He paused to get his breath back. "You've always taken good care of me. Of David and Phillip and Kim, too. Edith, you have the purest heart of anyone I know. Wear it and use it to tell my story after I'm gone. Will you do that for me?"

"Of course I will."

And there I was—an actress, a speaker, a writer—but I couldn't find the words to tell my brother how much his thoughts and this wonderful gift had touched me. I couldn't come up with the words to tell him how his faith and courage in the face of this awful thing had made me a stronger, better person. How he had made all of us who knew him stronger and better.

Maybe I would be able to explain it to him someday, I thought. Maybe someday I could return the favor and show him how much he meant to me.

15

My brother Terry was a tall, strong man, an athlete who loved raising quarter horses, training dogs, and reading western novels. Even with the best outcome, it appeared most of that was over for him now. I couldn't imagine how it would be for him, such a vigorous, active person, a man who made his living with his hands. Now he was powerless to do any of those things he enjoyed so much.

We had no idea it would be a seven-year ordeal.

When we took him back home from the hospital, I stayed with him as much as I could while still trying to keep my businesses and the foundation on an even keel. So did the rest of the family. Kim was there as much as she could be. So were Daddy, Mother, and Mother's husband, Tom. Dad and Tom built him a ramp so he could guide his electric wheelchair out of the sunken den and onto the rock-floored patio. There he could enjoy the warm sun and watch his horses as they grazed and ran around in the distant pasture. My son, Linc, was not even a teenager yet, but he gladly spent many nights sleeping in his Uncle Terry's bedroom, reading to him, fetching him water, helping him use the bathroom, and giving him sponge baths.

Something else had been going on in my life as well. My old high school teacher, Barbara Cashion, had reconnected me with my senior prom date, Mark Aldridge. He was now a high school coach and teacher, a handsome, gentle man. He was smart, too, an instructor in math and science and remarkably dedicated to his students. Mark could have made a lot more money in business or as an attorney, but he loved teaching and coaching young people, helping bring out the best in them.

It would not be accurate to call what we did "dating." After Terry's surgery, Mark and I spent most of our time together with my brother, doing all we could to make him comfortable and give him some quality of life. I figured anyone who would be so devoted to his girlfriend's invalid brother would make a good husband, so when Mark proposed, I accepted his offer of marriage.

We were married at a golf tournament we were putting on to support the Edie Hand Foundation. Terry was too sick to come to the wedding ceremony. We spent a short honeymoon together, but not before we visited at Terry's house, playing Scrabble and Rook at his kitchen table, trying to involve my brother in the games. He mostly sat in his wheelchair in his sunken den, though, listening to the Dolly Parton CDs my good friend, legendary music publisher Buddy Killen, had sent to him

When none of us were able to stay with Terry, we had a home health nurse or a friend or family member come in to take care of him. I felt guilty every time I left his place and headed back to work. What had Mother said about David when he was killed in the accident? "You should have been there with him!" When the self-reproach got too strong, I turned the horseshoe ring into a pendant and put it on the chain with the cross necklace my mother had given me before one of my own surgeries. I held it in my hand for comfort anytime I had to be away from him. Then, as soon as I could, I would drive back down to Burnout to help take care of my last brother.

Terry spent some time at a rehabilitation hospital in Birmingham trying to learn how to do what little he could with his waning strength. I knew it was hopeless, and I suspect he did, too, but it got him out of that house for a little bit. Still, it was upsetting to see him struggle with the simplest things: button a button, move the switch on his electric wheelchair, try to comb his hair, which had grown back gapped and uneven after the surgery.

It was awful watching Terry's powerful body

deteriorate. At least with David and Phillip, the end had come quickly. Terry, though, declined over seven long years, knowing all the time that the end of his journey was coming at him with an awful sureness.

For the most part, he handled it as well as anyone could have been expected to. But sometimes that temper of his still sparked. When even that seemed to wane, we knew it couldn't be much longer.

I was visiting him at the rehab hospital one day when his doctor, John Riser, came in to examine him. Dr. Riser had one of the best bedside manners I had ever known, but his face was somber when he nodded for me to step outside Terry's room for a moment. I knew whatever he was going to say would not be good. It had been a bad day already. I had cried most of the three-hour drive down from Nashville, begging God to give me the strength to handle the inevitable. So far, I saw no evidence He had heard that prayer, and I had the three-hour return trip and a long night's work ahead of me.

"Edie, I'm afraid he's going downhill fast. The

tumor is growing more rapidly and it won't be long now. There's nothing else we can do. We just need to make him as comfortable as we can."

I became dizzy and almost fell. I grabbed the doctor for support, and, bless him, he put his arms around me and held me. Somewhere deep inside I had harbored some hope that Terry would miraculously kick this thing, that he would one day climb back up on one of his horses and go galloping full speed off across the pasture toward the Indian mound, his long, dark hair blowing in the wind.

I had certainly prayed enough that he would. Now it was clear those prayers were not going to be answered either. Despair rolled over me.

For an instant, I wanted to lash out at someone, blame someone for putting my brother through this—the doctor, God, somebody.

"Edie, I know the frustration you are feeling," the doctor told me. "Just because we see it everyday, it's not easy for us either. God will help you. Don't give up on Him."

It seemed like he had been reading my mind.

His words did help. I just didn't know how long they could hold me together.

I'm not sure how, but I got through my goodbyes to Terry without breaking down. I showed him the pendant, and he smiled.

"I'll see you when you get back home," I told him.

"I'm ready," he answered.

"Ready?"

"Ready to go home."

I made my way past the other rooms filled with suffering folks, past families standing sad-faced in the hallways talking with doctors, and out to the hospital parking deck. By the time I was to my car, I couldn't see anything for the tears in my eyes. I was choking on the lump in my throat, and I didn't care who saw me. I pounded the roof of my car with my fists.

How could God take all three of my brothers from me? Surely He must know what they meant to me! And what had Terry done to deserve this suffering? There was no kinder, gentler man on the planet, until the tumor turned him at times into an angry man. He could hardly muster enough strength to hug me goodbye when I left his room.

I leaned back against the car and tried to breathe in some cool air, to calm down before I got behind the wheel and attempted to drive. I don't know what made me look down at that moment. When I did, I noticed a small, dirty piece of paper stuck to the bottom of my shoe. I also don't know why I reached down and pulled it loose. I could have just as easily stepped on it with the toe of my other shoe and kicked it away. I can't fathom what force kept me from crumpling it up when I did reach and get it. Or what power urged me instead to see what the scribbled handwriting on that raggedy little slip of paper said.

It was a small Post-it with an angel on it. Most likely it had once been pasted onto a gift on its way to be delivered to someone at the hospital. At the bottom was a type-set phrase that proclaimed, "I believe in the old rugged cross."

I smiled. That was a line from one of the songs

we used to sing on Grandpa Walter's and Grandma Alice's big front porch. It was one of Mother's favorites when she dragged me from bed to play the piano and sing for her folks.

There were handwritten words on the slip of paper as well. They were scrawled in a wavering, shaky hand. I wiped my eyes with the tissue I carried until I could read them.

They said: "Taste and see that the Lord is good; blessed is the man who takes refuge in him. Psalm 34:8"

I looked around the parking deck. There was no one around but me.

There could be no way that little slip of paper was an accident. It didn't land right there in that parking deck and get stuck to my shoe on one of the darkest days of my life simply by coincidence. At a time when my doubts were threatening to get the best of me, when there was no hope apparent to me, here was a sign that I still had a place to turn for sanctuary.

I cried all the way back home anyway, but they

were a different kind of tears. God had heard my prayers after all. He would provide some way for me, for my brother, for the rest of our family to handle what was about to happen if we only took refuge in Him. He would give us hope when we were most hopeless.

God would surely provide a way to cope with the rough places along life's ride, just as He had always done.

16

LINC AND I put up the live Christmas tree in Terry's den before we left for California. The apple had not fallen far from the tree, and my son was determined to make it as an actor. He was now living in Hollywood, and I was bound to do all I could to help him. I was going to take him out and introduce him to some people I knew. Besides that, I hated to have him out of my sight for too long.

Terry didn't say much as we sawed the trunk off the tree, trimmed the bottom limbs, set it in the stand, and then began hanging the family ornaments on the tree's branches. Usually he would be trying to supervise, telling us how to do it the best way, pointing out spots we missed, but not this time.

It was clear Terry's pain had become almost unbearable, and the medicine he was taking to blunt it left him listless and not very communicative. He had started to lose all of his fine motor skills and had trouble holding onto his comb to keep his hair in place or to grip a spoon to eat the soup I made for him. He was already in a wheelchair. His speech was slurred, and we had to write the alphabet on a pad and point to the letters to understand his sentences.

Mark finished hanging the decorations while we were gone on our trip, and he stayed with Terry when he could get away from his duties at the school. The football team was in the state playoffs and, if they kept winning, he would be tied up almost until Christmas.

I was only gone for one week, but the difference in my brother was obvious when I got back home and drove down to Burnout to relieve Mark, my

Mom, and the home health nurse. He now sat slumped to the side in his wheelchair most of the day as he half-watched the television or stared out the window as the same Dolly Parton songs played over and over. He had no interest in eating anything, not even the first experimental batch of Christmas cookies I made for him, using a recipe from a new holiday cookbook I was completing.

Kim and her girls, Kristi and Kayla, had moved into one of the bedrooms, and Mark and I usually stayed in another when we could spare the time to be there. Aunt Linda, who had tried to assist David at the scene of his fatal wreck and was at the hospital the night they brought Phillip in, had used up her sick days at the hospital, driving up to help us when she could, too. She had vowed she'd do all the good she could for this last Blackburn brother, even if she had to quit her job to do it.

Mother, who now lived in Indiana with her husband, Tom, came to visit when she could, staying a few days at a time, but when she was ready to go back home, she was ready to go. She called me.

"Edith, you need to come on back and stay longer with Terry," she said. "I have to get home."

"But Mother, I have a son to take care of, this new radio show I'm doing every day of the week, and the publishers are pushing us to finish the final draft of this book I'm working on."

She didn't seem to hear me.

"So . . . you can be here Saturday by lunchtime? Bring Linc and your tape recorder and your laptop computer. I have to get back home to Indiana, you see."

I suppose I could have gotten mad, but when I felt that old familiar emotion coming on, I prayed about it. God calmed me right down. I knew how much it hurt Mother to see Terry in the shape he was in and to know that he was steadily losing his battle for life. It was better for her to retreat, to go on back to her new life and not have to see Terry and his plight first hand.

Again, I had to be the strong one. If that was a part of God's plan, then I would just pack up my tape recorder and my laptop and my boy, and we'd come back and stay awhile with Uncle Terry. The radio station was understanding and let me do the show from the phone in Terry's parlor, patched through the control board at the station.

During those final, awful days, I stayed as busy as I could when I was not at Terry's, writing a book, *A Country Music Christmas,* and completing an album of music to go with it. My friend Buddy Killen had promised to help me tell Terry's story in a song, and he encouraged me to write a book about Terry and my brothers.

I know the laughter, the instincts to do the right thing, and the courage to keep riding in the right direction comes from all those I have loved and lost who are waiting and watching from the other side. For that reason, I am not afraid to take my last ride.

Whoever was there with Terry during those days took turns helping him to the bathroom, getting him from the bed to the wheelchair, bathing him, reminding him to take his medicine, trying to get him to eat something. Nobody said anything, but we all knew what we were really trying to accomplish. We wanted to keep him out of the hospital, to allow him to stay at home until after Christmas. Even though he never said so, we knew Terry desperately wanted to spend his last Christmas in the house he built, surrounded by his family.

We got almost daily calls from Dr. Riser. He had stepped outside his detached physician's demeanor to take a personal interest in Terry and his condition. He let us know we could move Terry to a hospital for his final days, but he never tried to talk us into doing it. He knew how much being there in his own place when the journey ended meant to Terry and his family.

17

THE END OF Terry Blackburn's journey came two days short of Christmas, a few minutes after the sun rose on another glorious Alabama morning. As usual, the sun came up over the Indian mounds, topping the cedars at the far end of the pasture like a bright Christmas star.

I was there on his bed beside him, holding him in my arms, when he died. My husband, my sister, Kim, and Terry's boy, Davey, were there, too. Aunt Linda was hovering over him, trying to make his last moments as comfortable as she could, just as she had done with my other two brothers who had died much too young.

There had been some talk of taking him back to the hospital in Birmingham when we knew the end was close at hand, but he would have none of it, even if it might have meant a few more days of life. He wanted to spend Christmas at home if he could manage it, and we didn't press the point. In the end, it really didn't make any difference. With the wonderful help of the hospice folks and his doctors and Aunt Linda, he was much better off right where he was, right where he most wanted to be at the end of his ride.

I held my baby brother in my arms as we experienced our last sunrise together. We remembered all those rides we had taken as children. At one point, I came right out and asked him a question that was heavy on my mind.

"Terry, can you see David and Phillip? Are they here? Blink twice if they are here and you can see them."

And he did. He blinked twice. We were all four together again. I knew he was telling me the truth because I had sensed their presence there myself.

Then Terry took his final breath. A strange, calming mist seemed to come into the room. Everyone in the room saw it, too.

Aunt Linda and the hospice nurse both maintained that they felt angels filling the room after he was gone. So did I.

I let him go then, physically and emotionally, and allowed his still, quiet body to sink back onto the bed. I stood, wiped my eyes, and then went out to the living room and sat down in Terry's favorite chair.

That's when I felt the hands on me. Gentle, soothing hands. Mother and Dad were across the room. The hospice nurse was with them now, comforting them. No one else was there. But I knew whose hands they were. It was my brothers, comforting me. I felt peace. In the middle of a storm, I felt total peace. And it came from those young men I loved so much.

We buried Terry on a quiet hillside not far from where we grew up and where we played together as children. He was placed in a plot right next to where David and Phillip lay. Each grave was marked by identical headstones but with different verses carved into their marble faces. The Hacker Cousins' graveside song "Go Rest High on That Mountain" still echoes in my mind.

Several tall oaks dot the cemetery, and if you rest on one of the benches that have been placed in their shade, you can see a stretch of the highway that runs on into Burnout. Beyond is a pasture where someone's horses usually graze and play among the pines and cedars when the weather is nice.

If you have a good imagination, you can almost picture yourself lying on your belly in the grass atop the Indian mound, your younger siblings lined up next to you. You can envision your horses, tied up and grazing patiently below as you watch the occasional car pass by on the highway and make up funny stories about the folks who ride in it. And if you have a good imagination, you can visualize you and your brothers lying there in the gathering dusk, spinning brilliant, hopeful dreams and scripting exotic adventures, all while you speculate about what wonderful things the road ahead might lead to for each of you.

You can do that, if you have a good imagination and if you sit there for a while on the bench under the oak tree.

I know.

I do, every chance I get.

epilogue

On Christmas morning, the day before Terry's funeral, I threw myself into the task of putting away what was left of all the food that friends and neighbors had brought by. I gathered up and tossed out some of the live flowers that were beginning to wilt and shed their petals on Terry's hand-sanded hardwood floors. Then I straightened up the house so even Mother would have been satisfied with the results.

Then there was nothing else left to do. Mark was

coming to get me that afternoon, and we were headed home to get ready for the visitation that night at the funeral home. Mark wasn't due for another couple of hours yet, and I flipped on the television. There were only a parade and some football games on, and I wasn't in the mood for either. The Christmas songs on the radio were too merry for my mood.

Finally, I pulled on my coat and walked down to the barn where Terry's horses were stabled, protected from the sudden deep chill that had descended upon us over the last couple of days. I wasn't sure where I was headed when I began my walk, but something seemed to be leading me toward the barn.

I fed the horses some sugar cubes and made sure there was hay available if they were hungry. Several people who were interested in buying them were coming by in the next few days. We hated to split them up, but knew they would be going to good homes, to places where they would be cared for almost as well as Terry did.

Even though it looked as if it was about to rain or snow at any minute, a sudden whim hit me. I saddled my brother's favorite horse, the one he had ridden on that warm afternoon only a week earlier. I ducked my head at the doorway and guided her out of the barn into the mist, then through the open gate and out across the pasture.

I still had no idea where I was going, so I mostly gave the animal her head. She seemed perfectly willing to drive.

We ended up beneath the bare limbs of David's and my special oak tree. Even without leaves, it seemed as tall and strong and healthy as it had decades ago when my brother and I sat in its cool shade and held our brother-and-sister heart-to-hearts. For a moment, I thought I could hear voices—maybe even our voices—but it was only the icy wind whistling through the naked branches of the tree.

From there I steered the horse on over to the base of the Indian mound, which wasn't far away. Unlike the oak tree, the mound didn't seem quite as tall and steep as it did when we were kids.

I dismounted, climbed up, and sat beneath one of the cedars that now covered most of the flat ground on top. It occurred to me that several of those trees would have made great Christmas trees, cut and trimmed and dragged back to the house behind the horse the way we used to do it.

It was cold and damp up there. The wintry wind now bore tiny grits of snow, and the darkening sky promised more would follow before long. But I sat there for a while anyway, listening to the fussing crows and to the distant whoosh of traffic on the highway down the way. I half expected to see Mrs. Magoo and her brood of kids pass by, her with her elbow stuck out and a cigar in her mouth and her kids hanging out every open window of her old station wagon. Or to hear the hoof beats of Polly and Spotted Cloud and Trigger, the whooping laughter of my brothers riding at a gallop across the far hill, coming my way chasing outlaws and rustlers, slaying dragons, and harassing King Kong.

I looked down at the horseshoe pendant Terry had given me the day after his first surgery. I had kept it with me because, with it around my neck, Terry was always with me, too. I took it between my cold fingers and reveled in its warmth and felt the spreading peace in my heart.

I had done what I had promised my brother in those darkest times that I would do. I had helped him make his last ride, exactly as he requested. That simple promise had given him hope when he had little else.

And I had kept my promise to God.

There had been plenty of times through the years when I questioned Him, angrily shook my fist at Him, wondered why He had given my family and me so much sorrow to handle, so many burdens to bear. Now I knew for certain why things had happened as they did.

It was just as Grandma Alice explained it to me.

"Edith, God gives us tests to make us stronger. He needs you to be especially strong because He has big plans for you. Don't let Him down, sweetie. Do your best and you'll get your reward here on earth. And then again in glory land, too."

God gave David a short but happy life. He led Phillip to His mercy before he suddenly took him home. He allowed Terry to be a tall, strong tree, an inspiration to others, including me. Then he gave Terry the strength to make that one last Christmas ride.

He allowed me to survive three bouts with cancer so I could be right there with my brother to help him to make that final ride.

Along the way, God gave me the insight to know, and some loving folks to keep reminding me, what His purpose was for me as I journeyed through this life. He blessed me with the ability and the opportunity to do good for as many other people as I could along the way. As Grandma Alice had explained so many years earlier, He had tested me mightily to see if I was up for the challenge.

There were tears in my eyes as the first big, wet flakes of snow began to fall, catching in the branches of the cedars like angel hair. I hurried back down the hill and climbed back up on Terry's horse. We galloped toward the house at a pace even David would have appreciated.

My ride was almost over, but I had a new

resolve. I had to make sure, starting right that minute, that I made the most of what was left of my life's journey. But I also had to make certain to enjoy the sights along the way. I owed that much to my Grandma Alice and to all the others who had gone on before me.

With the wind and snow in my face and this strong, beautiful horse carrying me toward home, I said a quiet prayer, promising God that I would faithfully do the best I could to do His bidding.

And I thanked Him with all my heart for allowing me to be there for that last, wonderful Christmas ride.

the end

Edie with her brothers Phillip, Terry, and David.

about the authors

Edie Hand's spirit for living is contagious. As a best-selling author and celebrity chef, a philanthropist, an actress, and a sought-after inspirational speaker, she puts her heart and soul into everything she does.

Hand grew up in the rural south as a member of the Presley family, and her modest upbringing taught her the simple joys of family, faith, and helping others. A three-time cancer survivor herself, she knows the importance of good health and reaching out to those in need of assistance. She founded the Edie Hand Foundation, a 501(c)(3) nonprofit organization, to raise awareness and money for special-needs children, especially those with motor dysfunction disabilities. Her tireless fund-raising efforts have benefited organizations including St. Jude Children's Research Hospital, Making Strides (A Division of the Birmingham, Alabama, Children's Hospital), The Christmas SPIRIT Foundation, and the Country Music Hall of Fame and Museum, among others. Edie currently lives with her husband,

Mark Aldridge, in Birmingham, Alabama. Her only son, Linc Hand, lives in Hollywood, California. Visit her website at www.ediehand.com.

Jeffery Addison is the pen name of an award-winning broadcast journalist, radio celebrity, and best-selling author. He has received major journalism awards from United Press International and the Associated Press and was twice named "Radio Personality of the Year" by *Billboard* magazine. Addison has authored or coauthored fifteen books, including an award-winning novel and a bestselling military thriller. In addition to his writing, he is a marketing executive and runs a full-service advertising and public relations agency. He lives with his wife near Birmingham, Alabama. Visit his website at www.jefferyaddisonbooks.com.

the songs

The narration and song on the following pages were inspired by the events depicted in *The Last Christmas Ride*. To obtain free downloads of both visit www.ediehand.com, then in the keyword box type TERRY.

The Last Christmas Ride

The scent of Christmas Day filled the air as the morning awoke us for our traditional ride
We saddled up our horses and celebrated each other my three brothers and I
Before the others awoke to share presents around the Christmas Tree
We'd go riding singing our Christmas carols—my three brothers and me

Joy and laughter filled the air as we ride through time and space to our favorite place
Time has passed seasons have changed as has the world we see
And now there are only three, since one took his special ride that foggy Christmas Eve
When he lost control on a country road and hit a fallen tree
Now he rides and sings his Christmas Carols with angels by his side
An empty saddle and the three of us will take our Christmas ride.

More years had come and gone another Christmas Day was dawn
The second one took a ride and, yes, he saw it coming
A speeding truck—a hit head-on left an awful sight
Two empty saddles would ride on when we took our Christmas ride

But faith kept us going though it was often put to the test
Just when I thought it's going to be alright and I'd laid it all to rest
The strongest one the one that was left, found his health began to fail
and over time he'd find his life become a living hell

For years I gave to him the gift of strength and a promise
that we would once again take a Christmas ride
He'd mount his horse and hold the reins as we rode side by side

Seasons have come and gone . . . bittersweet . . . as he spoke with just his eyes
as if to say . . . The boys are here . . . it's time . . .
I held him in my arms . . . I cried . . . as we took our last Christmas ride . . .
in our minds.

Written by Edie Hand and the late Buddy Killen

A Sister's Love

I remember my younger days in Alabama
And because of mother's health our sister was our momma
She tried hard to keep us all in line
While Daddy was on the road most of the time
Looking back she was a teacher and prankster
And those mud pies that she made boy that taste still lingers
Cause when we took a bite she laughed until she cried
When we got hurt she always held us tight

Chorus
She must have been sent from up above
She held us all together whenever times got tough
She was solid as a rock and always there for us
There ain't nothing in this world like a sister's love

We lived in Burnout...Alabam...can you believe
My brothers were always double dogged darin' me
So I took some paint and wrote plum on the welcome sign
But we got caught and lord she tanned our hides
We watched Elvis on a black and white TV
Picked cotton and we worked so hard in the stifling summer heat
We rode those horses through the drifting snow
Our BB gun really made her pony go

Chorus
She must have been sent from up above
She held us all together whenever times got tough
She was solid as a rock and always there for us
There ain't nothing in this world like a sister's love

Ronnie McDowell [Ronnie McDowell Music/BMI]
Edie Hand [Edie Hand Music/Grand Meadow Music/ASCAP/Adm ICG]
Joe Meador [Grand Haven Music/BMI/Adm ICG]